You'll laugh, you'll cry, and you'll cheer on Tylene Wilson, a woman who overcomes the odds to make her mark in a man's world.

This is more than a book about World War II or football—it's a novel about personal courage, perseverance, small-town life, and big-time dreams.

"A beautiful tale that stays in your heart long after you finish reading *When the Men Were Gone*. A delightful story, well written and touching. Looking forward to reading many more books by Lewis."
—Jodi Thomas, *New York Times* bestselling author of *Mornings on Main*

"Marjorie has written a wonderfully touching and beautiful story. . . . Tylene makes me laugh, cry, and cheer for her in ways I have not done in a long time. I only wish the real Tylene were here to see what Marjorie has accomplished. I was literally having chills. I look forward to the day her book launches into the world!"
—Diane Les Becquets, bestselling author of *Breaking Wild*

WHEN
THE MEN
WERE
GONE

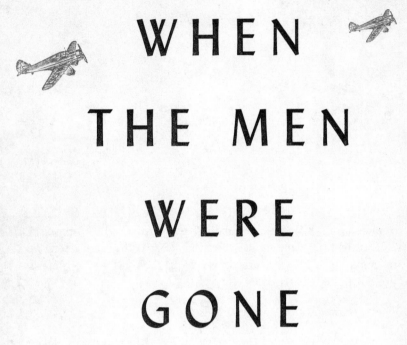

WHEN THE MEN WERE GONE

A Novel

MARJORIE HERRERA LEWIS

wm

WILLIAM MORROW

An Imprint of HarperCollins*Publishers*

P.S.™ is a trademark of HarperCollins Publishers.

WHEN THE MEN WERE GONE. Copyright © 2018 by Marjorie Herrera Lewis. All rights reserved. Printed in the United States of America. No part of this book may be used or reproduced in any manner whatsoever without written permission except in the case of brief quotations embodied in critical articles and reviews. For information address HarperCollins Publishers, 195 Broadway, New York, NY 10007.

HarperCollins books may be purchased for educational, business, or sales promotional use. For information please email the Special Markets Department at SPsales@harpercollins.com.

FIRST EDITION

Designed by Diahann Sturge

Library of Congress Cataloging-in-Publication Data has been applied for.

ISBN 978-0-06-283605-2
ISBN 978-0-06-286931-9 (hardcover library edition)

18 19 20 21 22 LSC 10 9 8 7 6 5 4 3 2 1

*With love, for my family and for Tylene's
grandniece Jean and mother, Mary*

PROLOGUE

Brownwood, Texas: 1910

My father and I climbed into our horse-and-buggy and began our three-mile trek. We had prepared for a squall moving through town, but we couldn't have known that the wind and rain would swirl so heavily that it would nearly toss me from the cart. At one point, my father had to catch me by my wrist to keep me on board. Just as he steadied me, the wind about swept away his cowboy hat. He clutched it, continuing to steer both horses with his left hand while holding his hat firmly on his head with his right. I hunkered down beside my father beneath the comfort and protection of my mother's homemade quilt.

"You okay under there, Petunia?" he shouted.

I pulled the cover back a bit, fought the rain from my eyes by squinting up at my father, and assured him all was well.

The only thing that bothered me about the weather was that it slowed us down.

Once we arrived at the high school, he lifted me from the wagon. "Perfect timing," he said. He squeezed the quilt to rid it of some water and then hung it over the buggy's wooden side. "Looks like the worst has passed."

He was right. The rain had stopped, the wind had subsided, and the Brownwood Lions had yet to kick off.

I ran to the field's entrance ahead of my father, a giant of a man in my eyes, though slender and probably not quite six feet tall. He had a distinguished look about him, with his deep-set blue eyes, wavy jet-black hair, and Grover Cleveland mustache, as my mother, with her keen sense of humor, had described it. I'd laugh when I'd hear her remind him, "Time to trim the Grover, George."

My father, slowed by a hip injury he had sustained a year earlier, eventually caught up with me. We entered and wove our way up the packed wooden bleachers to our regular spot, right off the press box near the far corner, if you're looking up from the field. We settled in, and when the Lions dashed out, I jumped to my feet. Soon after, the crowd of what I figured was nearly half the town's seven thousand residents also stood while the band led us in the school fight song:

For when those Brownwood Lions come down the field
They look a hundred per from head to heel . . .

And then the game began.

Shorty Wilkerson took the opening handoff. He was Brownwood's best running back, but on that night, he drove me crazy.

"Keep your knees high, Shorty!" I shouted. I knew he couldn't hear me above the cheers, the band, and the shouts of grown men yelling at the refs. But that didn't stop me. Although I was merely ten years old, my father and I hadn't missed a Lions football game together since 1907, and I knew right off that Shorty was far too sluggish.

"Come on, Shorty! Draw in your tackler and either speed up or slow down! Change your pace!"

I gnawed at my fingernails. I blamed it on Shorty. Then I turned to my father. "If he doesn't sidestep or accelerate, he'll never get into the open field."

The men around us began laughing.

"When are *you* going to call the shots out there, Tylene?" Mr. Periwinkle asked.

"I'll go down there right now if they'll let me," I said.

My father turned to the men. "Don't kid yourselves. She might just take over before the second half."

CHAPTER 1

1944

Wednesday

Hit a bull's-eye on a Texas map, and you've found my home. Brownwood, located in the heart of the Pecan Shell, three hours southwest of Fort Worth. It's a small town, where people praise Jesus, fix home-cooked meals for suffering neighbors, and play ball with kids in the streets. I've lived here since 1909. By then, my big sister, Bessie Lee, had already married and moved to south Texas, so when we arrived in Brownwood, it was just my father, mother, and me. Shortly thereafter, we were joined by Spot, our dalmatian. Well, he wasn't *really* a dalmatian; he was a mutt with spots. And he wasn't really ours. He belonged to the neighbors, but he was more often than not at our house. Brownwood is that kind of town. You share what you have. Sometimes that means sharing a dog. Other times, it means sharing the pain. We shared the pain last week when we got word that our football coach, Burl Young, had been killed in France while laying wire behind enemy lines.

Burl had been drafted in 1942, a week after his high school graduation, but the army opted not to take him once it discovered that he was the family's lone provider and the only son of a disabled father who had never recovered from a stroke. Burl stayed home and began coaching to provide for his father, Earl; mother, Mena; and two younger sisters. An assistant for one year, he had taken over the team last season soon after legendary local coach Gene Fox had taken a job in Dallas, his wife's hometown. But in the two years since he was drafted, Burl's sisters had proved they could care for themselves and their parents, too. Then one June morning when Burl read a newspaper account describing the heroics of the Normandy Invasion, he told his family he could no longer stay home. He packed a duffel and caught the first train out.

In his stead, Joseph Francis, a young fellow from a west Texas outpost who had answered a newspaper advertisement, had been hired in July. Two days after the publication of advertisements our principal, Ed Redwine, had placed in several Sunday-edition newspapers throughout central and west Texas, we got a call at the high school from a man who said he had seen the ad and had just arrived by train from a tiny town south of Lubbock. Mr. Redwine was off-campus attending a meeting, so I drove out to the station to pick up Mr. Francis. As I approached, I saw a tall fella, all gussied up, wearing a fedora and a pair of spit-shined shoes. He was carrying a small green suitcase in his left hand, and with his right hand, he was tossing a coin into a cup that belonged to a pair of little girls who looked like sisters—one playing an accordion and the other dancing to its melody. When I got out of my truck to greet him, he introduced himself.

"Joseph Francis, ma'am," he said as he tipped his hat. He said he had had a fine trip out and hoped the school had not yet found its man. Mr. Francis told me he had enlisted in the army in the fall of 1939, served for four years, and had come to town to begin his coaching career.

I brought Mr. Francis to the school, and for the following three hours he waited for Mr. Redwine. Upon arriving, Mr. Redwine hired the twenty-three-year-old Johnny-on-the-spot. I volunteered to show Coach Francis the lay of the land.

"This is a dream job for me, Miss Tylene," he said as we walked to the field house. "When I was a little boy, my dad introduced me to football, and I've been hooked on it since. Played three years for Post. Some of the best days of my life."

I told Coach Francis that I, too, had been taught the game by my father. We then discussed what football meant to a community, and I made it clear to him that while football reigns in Texas, there is no place better to be on a fall Friday night than in the stands of the Brownwood Lions football stadium—unless, of course, you're on the field.

"I guess that makes me the luckiest fella in Texas," he said.

Then just as unexpectedly as he had arrived, Coach Francis was gone. Last week, when he got word that his kid brother had been taken as a POW, he reenlisted.

SO ON THAT first Wednesday of September, there was no coach, no team, and no hope. Still, just as I had for every inaugural practice date in the three years since becoming the school's assistant principal, I moseyed on down to the field at three thirty. I expected to see nothing more than our cross-bars standing tall in each end zone hovering over an empty playing field like parents at the dining table waiting for their children to fill the seats between them. I wanted to sit for a moment. To imagine the boys preparing for the season. To deal with my emotions of fear and uncertainty—without a football season to look forward to, sixteen- and seventeen-year-old boys may prematurely go off to war.

When I arrived at the field, I was surprised to find two seniors, Jimmy Palmer and Bobby Ray Brashears, playing catch. As I sat on the bottom bleacher, neither appeared to notice me. Jimmy, the senior quarterback, had been designated captain during team meetings last spring. He was throwing deep to Bobby Ray, a senior flanker who had gained the attention of the University of Tulsa Golden Hurricane, a perennial New Year's Day bowl team. Jimmy and Bobby Ray were in blue jeans rolled up at the ankles, Keds sneakers, and plain white T-shirts, playing on an unlined field of grass, brown and beaten by the sun.

At one point, when Bobby Ray ran a route, Jimmy overthrew him, and the ball rolled end over end, skidding off the grass and across the dirt track, heading straight for the stands. It stopped directly in front of me. As Bobby Ray started my way, I picked up the football and gripped it tightly in both palms.

"Stay back!" I yelled. He stopped. I held the ball in my right hand and used my left hand to adjust both sides of my dress, then I kicked off my heels and stepped onto the field in my stocking feet. "Run five yards out and cut right!" I shouted. He appeared confused, but he did as I asked. I pulled the ball back in my right hand, and as I let it fly, my string of pearls slapped up beneath my chin. Bobby Ray caught the spiral in stride.

Stunned, Bobby Ray looked at me. "Nice pass, Miss Tylene! Where'd you learn to throw like that?"

"My father," I said. I adjusted my horn-rimmed glasses.

Jimmy ran toward us. "Wow, Miss Tylene! Any chance you can teach *me* to throw like that?" I was flattered for a moment, but mostly I was reminded of Jimmy's southern charm. I reached down to grab my heels, and at that second, Jimmy, Bobby Ray, and I heard a plane, and our smiles disappeared.

President Roosevelt had converted the town municipal airport and placed it under control of the Brownwood Army Airfield, and though its purpose was to train and prepare ground combat crews for overseas deployment, it was also used to receive the bodies of the central and west Texas deceased. Until the *Brownwood Bulletin* reported that week that Coach Young's body would arrive soon, no one had been certain when to expect his return. Not even his mother, Mena. But on the rare occasions when a plane was spotted making its way to our tiny airfield, folks were pretty sure a body would be aboard, whether it be from Brownwood, or San Angelo, or Big Spring. Knowing that Burl's body would be next, when Jimmy, Bobby Ray, and I looked up this time, we knew our coach was on his way home.

The boys and I walked off the field. I then jumped into my truck and headed for Mena's. I found her on her front porch swing, facing west in the sweltering heat. She wasn't crying. She was rocking slowly with her eyes locked on the cloudless blue sky. A couple of neighborhood women were leaving as I arrived.

"Hasn't said a word," one told me as we passed on the front yard walkway.

I was determined to wait my dear friend out, so I sat beside her. Back and forth on that swing, neither of us spoke. Finally, perhaps thirty minutes later, while her eyes were still locked skyward, she whispered.

"Best we go get him."

Mena had never learned to drive. Her husband, Earl, had suffered the stroke five years earlier, and in an instant my dear friend's husband had gone from someone who could spin a yarn with the best of them to silent and bedridden. Because his face was without expression and he could no longer speak, we could not have known if he was aware that the body of his only son, at last, was home. Earl stayed behind.

By the time Mena and I arrived at the airfield, nearly a hundred townsfolk had jammed into the hangar. Mena and I weaved our way through the crowd of mourners and stood silently up front as Burl's body, forever tucked away in a plain wooden box, was carried from the cargo bay. Across the way, I spotted Jimmy and Bobby Ray.

That night, my husband, John, sat at the kitchen table while I prepared supper. At six feet, two inches tall, he looked uncomfortable and oversized for our wooden kitchen chairs, which he and his auto shop buddy, Walter, had built about five years earlier. John had a slender but muscular build, likely because of all the heavy lifting required at the auto repair shop he purchased just months after high school. As I chopped the vegetables, we talked about Burl, and then the room fell silent for several minutes, my mind wandering in so many directions. Finally, in an effort to lighten the mood, I told John about the spiral I'd thrown to Bobby Ray.

"I suspect he'd never caught a spiral from a lady," John said, wiping sweat from his thick, wire-framed glasses. Then he smiled, and I went on to remind him of the first time we had thrown a football together—the first time *he* caught a spiral from a girl.

I was a junior in high school, working after class crunching numbers at the rolltop desk on the second floor of his auto shop, when he shouted up, asking if I wanted to take a break to toss a football outside. I agreed and ran down the tight, wooden spiral staircase to meet up with him. We stood about ten feet apart, and John, four years my senior and the most handsome boy I had ever met, flipped it to me. Underhanded.

John had cupped his hands in front of his gut and said, "Try to get it here." Instead, I dropped back. I looked left. Looked right. *Bam!* I smacked him with a pass John compared to a Jack Dempsey gut punch. We laughed at the memory.

"I looked down at the ball, and then up at you, and I knew," he said. "I was in love."

Thursday

The next morning, I drove to campus in my black Ford pickup. John and I had bought it off the lot in 1938, and I've kept it as clean as my freshly polished silver. Unlike a usual morning, I wasn't much in the mood for singing that day, but when my favorite song, "Ac-Cent-Tchu-Ate the Positive," came on the radio John had installed just a few months earlier, I figured it was just what I needed, so I cranked up the volume and joined in with the Andrews Sisters.

I approached the school and spotted Jimmy in the school parking lot. I gunned it, not so hard that I'd send gravel airborne—didn't want to hurt anyone or scratch the truck—but enough to get me to a spot in time to catch up. I parked, grabbed my handbag, and dashed. He had just lifted a box from his truck bed and was hightailing it to the field house.

"Jimmy," I shouted above the steady hum of machines churning at the nearby cotton plant, the largest in Texas west of Fort Worth.

He turned back and smiled as he saw me weaving hastily through the gravel in my one-inch pumps. He stopped and waited.

"Morning, Miss Tylene," Jimmy said. "Me and Bobby Ray intended to return the footballs after messing with them yesterday. We just forgot."

I wasn't concerned about the footballs. "I saw you and Bobby Ray at the airfield," I said.

Jimmy nodded and looked down. We began walking side by side toward the field house when Jimmy broke the silence.

"I got a letter from Stanley," he said.

Stanley, Jimmy's older brother, had played Brownwood football just three years earlier. He was a small but elusive running back, and the town considered him one of the finest to ever wear the Lions jersey. After high school, Stanley enlisted in the navy. Two months ago, he lost his left leg in the South Pacific. Amputated just above the knee. He was shipped stateside to the Naval Hospital in Bethesda, Maryland, and since then, Jimmy said he and his brother had exchanged letters almost weekly.

As he spoke, I looked down and saw Jimmy's letter jacket stuffed among the footballs, placed at the bottom of the box.

"Going to keep it in my locker," he said.

I nodded. "How's Stanley doing?"

"He was transferred to a Dallas hospital a couple weeks ago. Might get discharged sometime soon. My folks and I are keeping our fingers crossed."

"I will, too."

I'd known Jimmy's folks, Curly and Letta, since they were high school sweethearts. They'd graduated a year behind my husband, John, so they were seniors my freshman year, and like every freshman, I looked up to them in awe. Curly was a quiet guy, an intellectual type who never played sports. He was always tinkering with equipment, saying that someday he was going to invent something big. He was still on that journey. Letta was the outgoing popular girl, and I'd hear other seniors say they thought Curly and Letta were an odd combination. I didn't see it that way. I thought they were perfect together. Curly proposed to Letta on graduation night, and they'd gone on to have three children—Stanley, Jimmy, and a bright and always smiling grammar schooler, Lucy, a childhood victim of polio who struggled to walk.

Jimmy and I parted ways. He continued on toward the field house, and as I turned and walked toward the high school, I got to thinking about that letter jacket. Lying in a box.

I ENTERED THE school to the embracing smell of wooden lockers freshly painted red, the first time they'd been painted since they'd been constructed ten years earlier. I passed the glass trophy case and headed straight for Mr. Redwine's office. Like so many Brownwood residents, Mr. Redwine had been at the airport hangar to honor the arrival of Burl's body. He understood the pain. Mr. Redwine and his wife, Angie, had lost a son a year earlier, but not to the war. His name was Tim, although he went by Mit, *Tim* spelled backward. It was a nickname he'd been given in grammar school, because he always seemed to be on the wrong side of life. Then, at the age of thirty-six, unhappy, unmarried, and unemployed, Mit took his own life while visiting his parents' home.

Mr. Redwine never talked about Mit, though I know the memories of his only child are never too far away, and every death, whether associated with war, disease, or emotional struggle, affects Mr. Redwine in a personal way.

"Morning," I said as I entered his office, a room with space for nothing more than a desk and two chairs, identical to mine just one door down.

He had a copy of the daily newspaper on his desk. A photo with a story about Burl swept across the top of the front page, a reminder that Brownwood had become a bit of a dichotomy, depressed during the week and bustling on weekends, when families visiting soldiers stationed at nearby Camp Bowie filled the local hotels, including the twelve-story Hotel Brownwood, the town's tallest building.

A few years earlier, President Roosevelt had launched Camp Bowie, a military training site that housed thousands of American soldiers and thousands of German POWs just a mile outside of Brownwood. It was a city within itself. Seldom if ever did the men venture into town, but for occasions when out-of-town family members had come to visit. With its high walls and higher security, what took place within its walls was a mystery to the folks in Brownwood.

Still, despite the robust weekends, to the locals, Brownwood was a bit of a ghost town, much like so many other small towns since that December day in 1941. Wally's Drugstore, Hank's Appliances, Kramer's Bakery. Wally, killed in France. Hank, killed in Italy by friendly fire during a training drill. Kramer, a prisoner of war.

"When will it end, Tylene?" Mr. Redwine asked.

I shook my head. I couldn't find the words. I walked to the reception desk to pour myself a cup of coffee. Just above the coffeepot and taped to the wall was a typed version of the varsity football schedule, a reminder of our annual anticipation—second only to Christmas—where on fall Friday nights we meet at our town's single largest gathering spot: our football field. During the week, neighbors might be fierce competitors in business and classmates may jockey for grades, but not on those Friday nights, when the worries of life are washed away come kickoff. When our sons and brothers do battle for our collective pride and honor, we become one.

Still, with no coach, no team, and no season, I could not find it within myself to tear the schedule down. I had a feeling no one could.

Shortly after I left Mr. Redwine's office, I went to check on Moose Pecorella, a young man I'd hired for a three-day plumbing job at the school. Moose was a veteran. He had served in the National Guard for little more than a year and had been honorably discharged when he took shrapnel to his right hip. It left him with a limp and an inability to work at the cotton plant. Word around town was he had taken to drinking, but only in the privacy of his home, a place he'd inherited from his grandparents. It also was known about town that the war had left Moose fighting demons. He seldom shaved; his face looked worn and his hair unkempt. Still, he knocked on doors and handed out scribbled notes with his name, home address, and handyman abilities listed on them, making it clear to nearly half the town that he'd clean up if given a reason to. Despite his hardship, he was a fine young man with good intentions and a good heart. Though he had yet to secure full-time work, no one in town turned a back on him. He made his living doing odd jobs. That's how he ended up at Brownwood High that morning.

He was beginning day two of his three-day commitment when I found him lying on his back, on peeling red-and-white checkerboard linoleum, beneath a water fountain on the second floor. He had taken it apart and was halfway through the process of reassembling it.

"Discovered the cause of the foul taste," he said as he sat up. "Some pretty nasty rust. I also replaced a couple pipes that can be melted down. Still clean and good enough to donate. Will you be at the Boy Scout salvage drive tonight?"

"I'll be there," I said.

For a moment, neither of us spoke.

"I'm sorry about Burl, Miss Tylene. I know you and Miss Mena are good friends."

In truth, Mena was like a sister to me, more so than even Bessie Lee, who had left home when I was so young. I'd first met Mena when she sat across from me in fifth grade and had asked to borrow my eraser during arithmetic class. Actually, I was in fourth grade; she was in fifth, but Miss Trez taught two grades in one classroom, the only classroom in the school that had to combine grades to accommodate the overflow of children ages nine and ten. I was the new girl in school, having arrived from Zephyr that summer. Mena was pretty, and everyone admired her. She was tall for her age—nearly five feet, six inches—and had light-brown wavy hair that flowed to her shoulders. When we met that fall, she had a best friend, a girl with a name I'd never before heard—Coral, Coral Moon. Coral's family moved to College Station during the Christmas break, and I guess I filled in for her, because after that, Mena and I became inseparable. We double-dated a time or two during high school, played flute together in the high school orchestra, and even started out in college together, until she married and dropped out after our freshman year. I was her maid of honor, and later, John and I were Burl's godparents. Moose knew Mena and I were good friends. What he didn't know was that her pain was my pain.

"Seems every day brings more heartache, more sadness, Moose." And then the bell rang, and the hallway swelled with students scampering from one class to the next.

I headed back to my office, and like always, I passed the trophy case. I'd passed it hundreds of times over the years, but I had never stopped to look at it, to examine it and reminisce, until that day. And when I did, I saw Moose, his toothy grin front and center in the 1941 football team photo. I saw Shorty Wilkerson and was taken back to my childhood. I saw Alex Munroe, a classmate and lifelong friend who had gone on to referee college football games. I scanned the trophies and the photos and was reminded of why I have always loved this time of year. The hope of a good season, the enthusiasm of the student body, the unifying of an entire town.

My father had introduced me to football while we were still living in our old Zephyr home. In 1909, nine years after I was born, we left Zephyr, part of Brown County fifteen miles southeast of Brownwood, the county seat. We had moved in with my mother's parents on a vast Brownwood farm that had been in the Gray family for generations. After my grandparents died, we took over the farm and raised dairy cows. The land was also crawling with pecan trees, and I knew once the first pecan fell to the ground that football season was around the corner. It also meant homemade pecan pies, my favorite.

When late summer rolled around, all I needed was to hear my father say, "I saw a nut on the ground this morning," and I'd bust out of the kitchen's screen door, grab a bucket off the back porch, and scramble to the first pecan tree I could reach, singing the Brownwood Lions' fight song all the while. Still singing, I'd crawl on my knees and gather up pecans. I'd toss aside the nuts with cracks—those weren't good enough for my mother's homemade pies, but I knew they'd make a swell snack for the critters looking for a bite to eat. Sometimes, when my sister was in town, she would gather nuts with me, but she was close to a dozen years older, had married young, and had no interest in scraping her knees. Bessie Lee preferred to help Mama bake the pies. I enjoyed the baking, too, but gathering the nuts was just as fun. The briars and weeds beneath the trees didn't bother me. I considered a scraped knee a sign that a good pie would soon be on the way.

Once I had a bucket full of pecans, I'd haul the nuts to the house. Sometimes the bucket was so heavy, I'd crawl on my knees and push it. When I'd approach the porch, my dad would shout at the bucket, "Where'd you leave Tylene?" He claimed he couldn't see me. I'd shout from behind the bucket, "I'm back here, Daddy!" I can't remember if I thought he believed the bucket had left me behind or if I just played along with him. In either case, it was always good for a laugh. I'd gather pecans daily until I had harvested enough for my mother and the ground beneath the trees was mostly bare.

Shortly after I'd begun gathering the nuts, football season would arrive, and father-daughter time would begin. *Daddy time. Mama's pies. Football.* I particularly recall the 1912 season opener when my father and I rode my favorite horse,

Joe Drowser, an aging, mild pinto, to the football game. I could tell Dad was wondering why I was wearing an old bulky jacket that had long before belonged to Bessie Lee. He had taken one look at me, and his brow furrowed. It wasn't an angry look; it was a confused one. After all, it was probably near a hundred degrees outside. He didn't ask any questions. When we got to our seats in the stands, I pulled out two wrapped slices of pecan pie, one from each jacket pocket.

"Why am I not surprised, Petunia?" he said.

"Had no place else to stash them, Daddy. Want a piece?"

He laughed and shook his head. Told me to enjoy them. I ate one slice during the first half and the other during the second.

I wanted to smile at the memory as I walked back to my office, but because I was so concerned about the status of this football season, I couldn't.

WHEN I GOT home late that afternoon, I found John sitting at the kitchen table. Before the war had begun taking a toll on a few local industries, especially the automobile, it was rare to find him home before supper had been prepared. But in the last couple years, work at the shop had come to a near crawl, so John was getting home much earlier. Gas and rubber had been rationed because of the war, and fewer cars had remained drivable. What sustained the business was John's contract with Vern McSorley, a close family friend, who owned a fleet of trucks used to deliver milk throughout the state. Occasionally, John would threaten to close up shop and get into the hotel business, a bustling local industry during those war years because of the Camp Bowie population. He often referred to a popular five-bedroom boardinghouse opened by a local war widow for use by visiting families of Camp Bowie soldiers as a model for his new venture. But I knew he never meant it; he loved working on cars.

Still, lately, when I'd arrive to find John already home, he was typically poring over the bills. That was what he was doing that evening. And he was in a panic—his arms crossed against his chest, whether standing or sitting, had always been the giveaway. When I'd see him that tense, I'd rub his shoulders for a moment, which would inevitably lead him to packing away the bills and putting on an optimistic smile, just as he did that night. So as I warmed up a leftover chicken casserole—I had to eat quickly so as to return to the school for the Boy Scout's salvage drive—I mentioned that I, too, had to pay the monthly bills on behalf of my parents, who had been visiting Bessie Lee the past six weeks in south Texas. My father's ranch hand, Enrique Montano, was overseeing the family property. Enrique had been working for my father for many years, and I had no worries of the ranch's care. John and I also talked about the fond memories brought on by my stop at the trophy case.

"Brownwood hasn't canceled a football season since 1918," I reminded John. World War I was the reason. I was a senior in high school, and I clearly remembered the principal quoted in the newspaper at the time saying that canceling the season had been a mistake.

"I wish there was something I could do to prevent it from happening again," I said.

"There is," John said. "And it's been on my mind near constantly since Coach Francis left."

"What is it, John?" I asked. "What's been weighing so heavily on your mind?"

"Last night, when Walt and I were closing the shop, don't know why, maybe it was the creeper Walt was putting away after sliding out from under a DeSoto, but I got to thinking about how you and I met. You ever think about that?"

I had just lifted the fork to my lips, but I stopped and began to laugh.

I was fourteen years old when I heard through the grapevine that John's Automotive Garage was looking for a bookkeeper. John had graduated from Brownwood High a year earlier. He worked throughout high school as an auto mechanic. I knew of John only because he had once stopped by our family ranch to work on my father's truck. At the time, John had no garage, so he went from house to house fixing cars, polishing them up, and getting them back on the road.

I had heard that John was frugal and that when he graduated, he had the money to buy a dilapidated gas station once owned by a fellow named Leo Bernard. It had flourished under Leo's ownership for quite some time. But when Leo had died two years earlier, no one in his family had the skill or the desire to keep the station running. So it sat, a home for mice. Occasionally armadillos would visit, but John said that even they didn't stay for long. John told me the place was as filthy and inviting as an abandoned outhouse. Rusted gas pumps, spiderwebs with too many dwellers. And lots and lots of dirt. But despite the smells and the mildew, John said he

had a vision. He bought the place from Leo's family and converted it into the most popular garage in Brownwood.

I had just completed my freshman year of high school
when I arrived at John's Garage. I found John. He was tall,
dark-haired, wore wire-rimmed glasses, and had linebacker
biceps exposed by his short-sleeved coveralls. He was looking
under the hood of a black 1914 Chevy truck, the left side of
the hood open, resembling an accordion as it folded over onto
one side.

"I hear you're looking for a bookkeeper," I said. "I'm Tylene
McMahan. What does it pay?"

John turned to me, grabbed a rag, and began wiping his
hands.

"Fifteen cents an hour," he said.

"I hear the mechanics make thirty."

John stared as if wondering where this was going. "I need
a bookkeeper. I got no need for a mechanic."

"I'll do it for the extra fifteen."

"I'm not sure you know how to keep books. Why would I
give you an extra fifteen? Besides, I don't have it."

"Oh, yeah?" I said. I looked around. The place was nice.
There were plenty of cars, and the workload looked like it
would keep John busy for months.

"I can do the books. I'll start now, but with the extra
fifteen."

John looked dumbfounded.

"I'll give you an extra two."

"Fifteen."

"Five."

"Fifteen."

"Seven."

"Fifteen."

"Tylene, I can't afford you."

I turned and slowly began to walk away. I'd gotten as far as the garage door when John shouted, "Twelve."

I stopped and turned back. "Where's my office?"

Three years later, John and I began dating. Late into my senior year, I was still doing the books and getting close to high school graduation. John had hired two more mechanics, doubling his total to four. He had expanded the garage to meet the demand, and he had all the finest equipment.

One afternoon, when the men were out to lunch, my curiosity had gotten the better of me. I lay down on the flat *thing* the men used to slide underneath the cars, something they call a creeper. I slid myself under, just to see. *Wow. What a mess of stuff. Fascinating.*

I lost myself in the maze of metal. So focused, I never heard a sound. Then I saw shoes. Boots, to be exact. John's boots. I recognized the worn black leather that rose above his ankles, the top of the laces untied.

"Tylene," John said softly. "I need to ask you something."

I slid out from under the car, still lying flat on the roller *thing.*

"I've been thinking," John said. "We've known each other for almost four years now. Been dating the last year. You're getting ready to graduate. I'm thinking we might want to get hitched. What do you think, Tylene? How about getting married?"

I stared at him. Then I slid back beneath the car.

I whispered from below the chassis. "No."

I could see his boots pacing.

"Tylene, I have the business. It's going great, and I have at least enough money to buy us a house. I can take care of you. Just think about it, Tylene. Take your time. You don't have to answer now. I can wait until you roll out from under the car. By the way, why are you under the car?"

"John, maybe someday," I said, knowing John could see only my feet, which were covered in peach-colored heels, the kind my friends would say were worn by first ladies and princesses. "You know I only took this job to save for college. I don't need to be taken care of. I'm going to be a teacher, remember? I have things to do before I think about getting married."

Eleven years from the day we met, we married.

Now, together in our kitchen, John again left me dumbstruck.

"Will you do it, Tylene? Will you coach the boys? I think he would have wanted you to."

"Are you crazy?" I asked. I was so stunned I didn't even think to laugh at the outlandish suggestion. I grabbed John's empty plate from the table, picked up my own, and got up to put them in the sink. As I began to prepare the soap and water for cleaning, I turned back to John, who had gotten up and was standing right behind me.

"You better cut down on your exposure to gas fumes," I said. "It's doing a number on that brain of yours."

"Tylene, I'm serious."

"John," I said, shaking my head. I placed my palms on the sides of his face and kissed him gently on the lips. "It's official. You've plumb lost your mind." I turned back and continued washing the dishes. Without looking back, I said, "You do know there's one problem, one huge problem, right?"

"The lady thing. I get it," he said. "But you can do it, and you know that as well as I do. Hell, you could coach the Longhorns to a national title if they'd give you a chance."

I could feel the passion in his voice, so I turned toward him. He looked into my eyes as sure as he ever had. "Coach? Grease monkey? What's the difference, Tylene? No one knows you better than I do, and I say do it. I know you can, and, after a few days, the whole dang town will know it, too."

"Grease monkey?" I asked.

"I knew you tinkered on a few trucks."

He was right; I had.

"Let's leave it at grease monkey, John. I'll find our football coach."

He then kissed me on the forehead and left the room. I finished the dishes, and we left for the scout drive.

UPON ARRIVING AT the salvage drive, John and I found a packed parking lot—another reminder of how our town, which had swelled upward of fifteen thousand, banded together during times of need. John and I headed in different directions—John caught up with Vern McSorley and the school's handyman, Wendell Washington.

Vern and his wife, Mavis, were our dearest friends, and John and I often spent Saturday nights playing dominoes at either their home or ours. Vern was a tall, large man and somewhat intimidating. He had never run for public office, but he pulled sway on all the biggest decisions in town. He was well respected, and all business during the week, but on Saturday nights, over dominoes, he'd unleash a sense of humor that I suspected would have left Jimmy Durante envious.

Wendell, the high school's handyman and groundskeeper, was from Pennsylvania. His kin, originally from Mississippi, found freedom in the North, aided by the Underground Railroad. Wendell arrived in Brownwood in 1942 when his son was stationed in Camp Bowie. Wendell often said that he had just enough money to get to Texas to see his son but no money left for a train ticket home. I've always suspected he never intended to return to Pennsylvania, that the memories of his wife and young daughter, who perished in a house fire years earlier, cut too deep. Wendell's son married soon after his discharge less than a year ago and moved to New Orleans, his wife's hometown. Wendell had made Brownwood his home.

Wendell, Vern, and John joined the other men in a parking lot corner designated for the collection of rubber, typically tires no longer drivable, and scrap metal. Boxes also had been set up to collect tin cans and various forms of aluminum.

Although the Boy Scouts sponsored the drive, mothers of current and former scouts organized the collection of paper products. Mena had organized this year's paper drive, but with Burl's funeral set for the next day, she had handed the reins over to Mavis, who was not only a former scout mom but was the high school freshman composition teacher. Mavis also knew Mena's pain. Vern and Mavis lost their son at Pearl Harbor, and since that day, Mavis had sought every opportunity to keep herself busy. Her biggest fear, she'd said, was having nothing to do.

I'd known Mavis since middle school. She was a kind but timid woman, small-framed and no more than five feet tall. She was often overshadowed by Vern's loud and domineering personality, but it suited Mavis. Because we had developed a friendship at only thirteen years old, I had come to understand that, even as a schoolgirl, she preferred a place in the shadows.

I hightailed it into the gym to find Mavis and dozens of other ladies collecting and organizing the paper products, including cardboard milk cartons, cardboard boxes, and newspapers.

Two years earlier, Boy Scout troops across the country had begun sponsoring drives, brought on by labor shortages that resulted in reduced quantities of virgin pulpwood. Paper products were needed for several purposes, including the boxing of K rations, artillery shells, and canned goods. Metal was needed for building airplanes.

Brownwood Boy Scouts sponsored drives twice a year. The drives tended to uplift the community, providing an opportunity to contribute to the war effort—something other than sending their sons and fathers off to battle. As volunteers continued to pour into the gym, I took a twenty-minute break to tutor three students who had counted on me every first Thursday of the month.

Typically, three seniors struggling with English classes—
Bobby Ray, Lula Ann, and Katharine—arrived at my house by
six o'clock for a one-hour tutoring session. All three seniors
struggled with literature and composition, so late in their
junior year, I began tutoring them even though as assistant
principal, I no longer taught English. A week into their senior
year, we all picked up where we'd left off, only on that night
we had planned to meet in my office and keep it brief.

The class was reading *Little Women,* and Louisa May Alcott's
writing must have resonated with them because they—the two
girls, at least—said they were pleasantly surprised by the assignment. Bobby Ray said nothing, but I knew he enjoyed the
book because he wasn't sitting back yawning as he had so
many times before. I also knew he would never admit to enjoying the book. Certainly wouldn't want word to get out. But
he appeared as engaged as the girls. Though he didn't speak,
he sat up straight and leaned in on the discussion.

About to wrap up the session, Bobby Ray reminded me of
the spiral I had thrown to him a day earlier.

"I just never seen a lady throw like that," Bobby Ray said.
"You got quite an arm there, Miss Tylene."

"I've been practicing since I was about five," I said. "I
always knew I had no playing days to look forward to, but
it's a shame you don't now, either. How are the boys holding up?"

"Not good," he said.

I wasn't surprised. I just shook my head.

With the need to return to the drive, I concluded the session
by asking all three to give me one word that described why

they most admired the *Little Women* character they collectively named as their favorite: Jo.

"Different," Lula Ann said.

"Independent," Katharine said.

Bobby Ray remained silent.

"Bobby Ray, what do you most admire about Jo?" I asked.

"If I have to pick, I guess, *strong*. I kind of like that," he said.

We began to part ways. Bobby Ray told me he'd planned to meet up with two of his buddies, seniors Roger Duenkler and Kevin Mutz, but hadn't seen them. He asked if I had. I hadn't.

THAT NIGHT, JOHN and I were driving home when we saw Wendell's truck, a 1927 Chevrolet Capitol 1 with a hardwood-sided bed he'd reconstructed himself. The truck was built for crop fields and dirt trails and was the only one in town with its wooden sides painted red, so it was easy to spot. Wendell had parked in front of the Duenkler house. While passing by, I glanced over and saw Roger with his head bowed. Wendell appeared to have been giving Roger an earful.

CHAPTER 2

Friday

Entering the school building, I caught a glimpse of Roger near his locker located down the hall. It wasn't difficult to spot him among the crowd; he was the only student wearing his boiled wool letter jacket with a chenille *B* patch sewn onto its left breast. I walked his way and signaled for him to meet me in my office.

"Roger, why did Wendell take you home last night?"

"You heard?"

"Tell me what I have to know before word gets to Mr. Redwine."

Roger didn't speak. He also looked away from me.

"Roger?" I asked again.

After a brief pause, Roger turned toward me and looked me straight in the eyes.

"I got into my dad's whiskey cabinet and stole a bottle. Then me and Kevin snuck out of the scout drive. We weren't causing no harm, Miss Tylene. Just drinking out behind a tree. Mr. Wendell saw us. He ordered us to his truck. Kevin's dad saw us getting into the truck and took Kevin home."

"Roger, it's near a hundred degrees outside and not much less in here. You're sweating profusely and wearing your letter jacket. Why?" I asked.

Roger looked at me, then down toward the floor and whispered, "It's football season, ma'am."

"Roger, I'm patient. Just be honest with me."

He made me wait. Finally, he took his jacket off, and I nearly froze at the sight of welts and bruises.

"Certainly Wendell didn't do that to you."

"No, ma'am. My dad. Took a switch to me the moment I walked in the house. Didn't even know what I had done. He'd just seen me get out of Mr. Wendell's truck and figured I was up to no good."

I was horrified. Although I knew of his father's short fuse, I couldn't have imagined he was capable of such brutality, not on his own son. I had gone to high school with Roger's dad, Gil, who was known back then for his short temper. His nickname was Moonshiner. Originally just Moonshine, but when anyone else fired up an illegal still, he'd land a hay-maker smack-dab in the center of the fella's right eye. Gil was a southpaw, and folks knew if anyone was seen about town with a right-eye shiner, it had come courtesy of Moonshiner. This was my first indication that Moonshiner was leaving marks on Roger, too. My first thought was to call Gil and have him come to the school.

"Please don't, Miss Tylene," Roger said. "I know my father. He'll tell you what you want to hear, but it won't change a thing at home."

I was left dumbfounded. I knew Roger had gotten into trouble because he had found himself with nothing better to do. Although I knew I had no power to change Gil, I knew I did have the power to keep Roger out of trouble.

"Have you seen Kevin?" I asked.

"Yes, ma'am. He's fine."

Once Roger put his jacket back on and left my office, I went looking for Wendell. I found him in the chemistry lab, where Mr. Hightower was explaining a blockage in the sink.

"We're just about done," Mr. Hightower said as I entered the room. I knew Mr. Hightower had the weekly faculty meeting to get to, so I waited. Once he left the lab, Wendell turned to me.

"Saw you and Mr. Wilson pass by last night," he said.

"Have you seen Roger today?"

"No, ma'am."

"Got the switch."

Wendell looked down and shook his head.

"I couldn't just let it go," he said.

"You did the right thing, Wendell. What did the boys say?"

"Said they was talking about getting out of here. Got no reason to stay. I'm pretty sure if nothing changes, they be signing up early. Said they ain't afraid to lie about their age if their daddies don't sign off."

Wendell had served in the National Army during World War I. As a member of the Ninety-Second Infantry, he fought in France in 1918 on the Western Front—part of the Hundred Days Offensive in the Battle of the Argonne Forest. Wendell had told me tales of training in the trenches and of life on the front line. He was eighteen, living in Scranton, Pennsylvania, when he was called to war, and he struggled with the thought of the senior boys signing up early.

"Ain't no place for no seventeen-year-olds," he said.

"Same could be said for Burl's funeral. Will I be seeing you there?"

"Yes, ma'am. Got to pay my last respects."

"You're a good man, Wendell," I said.

I returned to my office, finished some paperwork, and then headed to Mena's home, where she and her daughters—Doris and Sally—were preparing for a reception to follow Burl's burial, scheduled for that morning at eleven.

I arrived to find John and Walter unloading tables and chairs from a truck bed. Mena had told us she had no idea of what kind of turnout to expect, but John and I figured it would be in the hundreds—upward of three hundred—so John put word out to families to drop portable tables off at his auto shop.

Mena had a modest house but a large backyard, so once John and Walter had the tables and chairs set out back, I began to lay out the tablecloths that I'd borrowed from a number of teachers. I'd also collected several vases, so I placed a small flower in each as table centerpieces.

While I set up outside, Mena and her daughters arranged the inside, making space for meals the guests would bring and opening up the rooms by pushing furniture against the walls.

Once we had the house ready, I left for home so I could change into the black dress I'd become accustomed to wearing for funerals of our fallen friends. Burl's funeral would mark the sixth time I'd worn the dress within the last four months. Each time, another layer of anguish added to it. Though I loved each of our fallen soldiers, Burl was more deeply personal. My godson.

I remembered the day that Burl was born. Mena had Earl stop by our house early that morning.

"Tylene! Tylene!" Earl shouted while pounding on our front door shortly after sunrise.

Still in my robe and slippers, I dashed to the living room and opened the door.

"It's a boy!" he said.

"Earl, you darn near scared me out of my wits!" I said. And then I called for John, and I asked Earl to come inside.

John joined us and congratulated Earl on the new addition.

"Mena couldn't wait for y'all to know," Earl said. "Asked me to hightail it here just hours after Burl was born."

"Burl. That's beautiful," I said.

"A family name?" John asked.

"Mena's father. He passed on before she was born, so she

swore if she ever had a son, she'd name him after him. Makes her feel close, connected in a way, to both of them."

I offered Earl a cup of tea, but he said he couldn't stay. He had a few more stops to make. I hugged him and told him I'd be heading to the hospital just as soon as I could. I still had to get ready for the day and fix John's breakfast.

Later that morning, I walked into Mena's hospital room. She was sitting up in the bed, holding Burl tightly.

"Don't think I've ever lived a happier day," she said to me before I could say hello. "Want to hold him?"

I took Burl in my arms, and while I was looking down at him, Mena surprised me.

"I've been wanting to ask you this since the day the doc told me I was going to have a baby. Will you and John be his godparents?"

Still looking down at Burl, I said, "We'd be honored." I looked up at Mena and smiled.

From that moment on, Burl had held a special place in my heart. Never did I imagine that one day I'd be driving to his burial.

I arrived at Greenleaf Cemetery just moments before John did. We joined up in the parking lot and walked to the burial site together. We had arrived with the early crowd and found a seat just behind Mena and the girls, who were already seated. Failing health had forced Earl to remain at home.

Slowly, the seats behind us filled. By the time the preacher began his opening remarks, I figured more than five hundred townsfolk had gathered to honor Burl's life. Ranchers, business-men, mothers, teachers, commissioners, and mayors—both of Brownwood and nearby towns. The largest cluster was of students, including football players who wore their jerseys to honor their fallen leader. The high school had loaded up buses so students could attend.

Just minutes into the ceremony, the preacher turned the microphone over to Jimmy.

"Coach Young was a hero to me," Jimmy said. "Not only for his sacrifice on the battlefield, but for his sacrifices for his family and for us. Leading up to my senior year, me and my fellow seniors looked forward to playing our last year for Coach Young."

Jimmy then turned toward the casket, draped in the American flag.

"Coach, I'll never forget the day you named me captain. You said, 'Jimmy, I trust you.' I'll never forget that, Coach Young, and I'll never forget you. You will always be my captain, and I'll miss you for the rest of my life. We will all miss you, Coach. God rest your soul, O captain, my captain."

Jimmy turned to his teammates as if looking for comfort. Bobby Ray and Roger walked up and hugged him. Jimmy then returned the microphone to the preacher, who went on to extol the virtues Burl displayed in choosing to fight for his country.

"We don't know what drives evil in our world, but we do know Burl gave his life fighting it," he said. That was about all I heard from the preacher. I was sitting so close to Mena that her sobbing drowned out much of what he went on to say.

She and her daughters were so shaken that I tried to remain composed in the event that they needed me. But once taps began, I knew I could no longer hold in my emotions. When the soldiers played the final note and lowered the bugles to their sides, I was overcome. First my infant son. Then my godson. *Enough,* I thought. My resolve was heightened. Through my tears, I promised myself: The senior boys would stay home. Their turn for duty would come soon enough.

Later that afternoon, I stopped in on Mr. Redwine.

"The boys need to play," I told him. "Keep the boys out of war, out of trouble, and out from under a switch."

"Switch?" Mr. Redwine asked.

Before he could say anything more, I reminded him of what FDR had said when Major League Baseball considered shutting down in January 1942, a month after the attack on Pearl Harbor: "'Play ball.' That's what FDR said, Mr. Redwine. He said the country needed it, and he was right. Now we need to play ball. The boys need football, and the school needs football."

"Tylene, you know I take no pleasure in canceling the season. But you know as well as I do, the men are gone. There is no coach out there, Tylene. No coach."

I thought of what John had suggested the night before, and especially how I had responded.

"With all due respect, Mr. Redwine, I refuse to believe that. I know it. I know there is *one* coach out there. I just have to find him. And I promise you this, I *will* find him, and he *will* be on board by Monday morning."

I then set out to form a committee of teachers I knew understood the value of football, even if they didn't understand the game itself. My first thought was to corner a few teachers as they entered or exited their classrooms, so when I spotted Miss Ruth Mary entering her home economics class, I weaved my way through the rush of students heading to their lockers and caught up with her. I explained what I was looking for.

"I know nothing about football, but count me in," she said. I was overjoyed, and still, I instinctively made a mental note that the O'Keefe & Merritt range she had begun fiddling with as we spoke was in need of repair.

I had just stepped out of Miss Ruth Mary's classroom when I spotted Mr. Grassly, the physical education teacher and track coach, talking with a student wearing a scout uniform and walking in my direction. Mr. Grassly was my next target. I was elated when he agreed. Mr. Grassly was so highly respected that if he was on board with a project, several other teachers typically followed suit.

That proved to be the case this time as well. I got our biology teacher, Mr. Durr, to agree, followed by Mr. Beekner, who taught Spanish. I was confident I had formed the perfect committee because, as I had expected, no one I spoke to wanted to see the football season canceled. By three thirty, I had formed my five-member committee—three men and two women, including myself. We met in the teachers' lounge, but before we began to brainstorm, we bowed our heads and said a prayer in memory of Burl.

"Amen" was followed by silence. I let it remain silent for about a minute, and then I had to change the mood.

"I told Mr. Redwine we'd have our coach in place by Monday," I said. "So what are we looking for?"

"A man," said Miss Ruth Mary. Then she smiled. "I told you I know nothing about football."

"Actually, that's probably about all we can hope for in two days," Mr. Durr said.

"Yes, we need a man," I said. "But just as important, he has to know football. Should we require experience?"

"Not much," said Mr. Grassly. "The way I see it, he has to understand the game, know the boys, and not make any changes. Can't be starting from scratch with the opener just two weeks away."

Mr. Grassly was smart and practical, and also right, in this case.

"Agreed," I said while opening the local telephone book. "Any suggestions? Names?"

"Bobby Ray's uncle might make a good coach. He hasn't missed a game in twenty years," said Mr. Beekner, who had graduated with Bobby Ray's uncle, Lester Brashears, and had remained friends in the years since.

"But does he understand football?" I asked. "Any reason to believe he can coach it?"

"I know he played it. He was a noseguard, or tackle, or something on the line back in the twenties," Mr. Beekner said. "He may not know much about the skill positions, though. Could be a stretch to consider him, but why not?"

"I'll put him on the list and talk to him later this evening," I said. "Anyone else?"

"I reckon Andy, the tall fella who works at the hardware store, played football. Not sure, but he's got the look," Miss Ruth Mary said.

"The look?" I asked. "What's the look? All I know is he's big, and he never smiles."

"He never played," Mr. Durr interjected. "He's just a mean fella. Don't put him on the list."

"How about Alex Munroe?" Miss Ruth Mary asked.

Alex and I had graduated from high school together, although by then, I had known him for several years. I met Alex when we were both ten years old and sat beside each other by chance at a Lions' football game. By halftime, we had engaged in a battle of football wits. I had held my own, and in the years since, we had become great friends. He played for the Lions when we were in high school. He wasn't a star; he was a student of the game and has always loved it as much as I have. I was certain Alex would make an excellent coach, but he and his wife, Judith, had moved to Abilene, where last year Alex had accepted an appointment teaching history at McMurray University. He also had his weekends booked—traveling throughout the state as a college football referee. Because he had remained one of my dearest friends, I knew without a doubt that he had no extra time.

One by one, we ran through the telephone book and reviewed names.

He knows football, but he works an eighty-hour week.

He travels for work. Out of town too often.

He's more of a basketball man. Loves football, though. Can't coach it.

He enlisted two weeks ago.

He enlisted a month ago.

He enlisted yesterday.

An hour later, the telephone book had more red ink scratched across it than a ninth-grade essay. I walked to my office holding an unreadable phone book and one piece of paper. Scribbled across the top, it read: Bobby Ray's uncle, Lester.

I grabbed my purse and walked toward the school's exit. I was about to pass the trophy case, when, like I had the day before, I stopped to reminisce. Through smudged fingerprints on the glass, I glanced at a pair of well-worn cleats, yellowing newspaper clippings, and bronze trophies commemorating former athletes and seasons. I saw the 1919 and 1920 schedules and results—the only two seven-win seasons in school history. As I was about to turn to leave, the corner of my eye drew me back. I zeroed in to get a better look. Front and center, number 42. I crumpled the sheet with Lester's name on it and tossed it into the trash just before leaving the building. I jumped into my truck and headed to see Moose.

"MISS TYLENE," MOOSE said as he welcomed me into his modest clapboard-sided home, its chipped wooden floors creaking with each step. "Sorry about the mess. You know I've been looking for work. Hasn't left much time to tidy up."

I ignored the living room clutter, though I couldn't help but notice the newspaper pages strewn on the sofa, beer bottles on the floor, and dirty dishes on the coffee table. Moose cleared a spot for me on the sofa, an old Louis XVI that I was certain his grandparents must have purchased at the turn of the century.

"Moose, it's been what, a few years since you played Brownwood football?"

"Yes, ma'am," he said. "Best days of my life."

He then asked me if I'd like a glass of water, and I accepted. When he returned, I had cleared a space for him beside me.

"Have you ever thought about coaching?"

"Coaching?"

"As you know, the season's been canceled, but maybe it doesn't have to be. Not if we find a coach."

He stroked what appeared to be about a three- or four-day growth on his chin, looked at the floor, and then stood up and began pacing slowly, his limp pronounced from little more than an arm's length away.

"Why me?"

"I passed the trophy case as I was leaving work today, Moose. I was reminded of what you've meant to Brownwood football."

"I'm flattered, Miss Tylene, but I ain't never run a practice. Wasn't much disciplined when I played, neither. I'd love to help; you know I would. But I think you're talking to the wrong man."

"Moose, I'm talking to the *only* man."

He remained silent.

"Sometimes in life," I said, "we find ourselves in situations we never anticipated, and we end up asking ourselves exactly what you just asked: 'Why me?' But you know what, Moose? The boys need to play football, and they can't do it without you."

I waited.

"Canceling. Wouldn't be right by the seniors," Moose said. "But if you need an answer now, I got to say no. I just ain't prepared for that. Never ever thought of coaching."

"What are you afraid of?"

"I never said I was afraid. I just ain't no coach."

"No, you're afraid. I'm sitting in your house, Moose, and I see it in your living room. I see the beer bottles. I see the clutter. And now, I see it in your face. Tell me why you are afraid."

We stared into each other's eyes.

A long pause followed his words. Finally, Moose said, "Look at this place. It's a mess. I'm a mess. I'm no leader, and I ain't never been no role model."

I got up and stood in front of Moose.

"I've never gone off to war," I said. "I've never been in-jured at war. I've never come back home hurt, alone, and scared. But now that I've been in your home, and with God as my witness, Moose, I believe you need the fellas just as much as they need you. If you trust me, you'll be fine."

"No disrespect, Miss Tylene, but what makes trusting you good enough to turn me into a football coach?"

"I know football," I said. "Learned it from my father. I love and respect the game, and I'll support you in every way.

"How about this?" I asked. "Run practice this week. Each evening, we'll sit down and talk. Let me know what's working and what isn't. If you like what you're doing and if you don't. Can you make that work for five days? Five days, Moose? All I ask is that you give me five days."

"Five days? I suppose that's not unreasonable," he said, scratching the back of his right ear. "But I still ain't ready to commit. I got to think about this. To be honest, your knock at the door woke me up. I still need to clear my head and take this all in."

"How much time do you need?" I asked.

"You need a coach by Monday?"

"Look, give me a call when you're ready. But, Moose, I'm planning on meeting you at the field house Monday morning, eight o'clock sharp."

I HEADED HOME, and when I arrived in my neighborhood and rounded my street corner, I found comfort in the view of my three-bedroom white wood-sided house. I slowed down as I entered the dirt driveway that led to the garage in the back of the house so I could peek at my redbrick-framed petunia flower beds. Satisfied that my favorite flowers were in fine shape, I parked in the garage and sat in my truck for a moment. I wanted to be alone, to think about Burl, and to collect myself after such a stressful day. A few minutes later, I stepped out of the truck, closed the garage door, and entered the house through the kitchen.

Once inside, I realized I was not only emotionally spent but physically exhausted and yet, surprisingly, also energized. Though the day had taken a toll on me, in the end, the possibility of having Moose on board left me with hope that the boys would get their season. I was focused only on putting my house shoes on and getting dinner started, when the smell of barbecue ribs reminded me that I had the "night

45

off." Although John and I had acknowledged the big day earlier that morning, I had since forgotten that it was our eighteenth wedding anniversary.

Traditionally, John cooked ribs for each anniversary, his specialty, taught to him by his father. I loved the sauce John whipped up for the barbecue. He wanted to keep the sauce his gift to me, so he had been steadfast in his refusal to share the recipe. Knowing that, I've never pressed him for it—at least not after having tried the first few years we were married to get him to share the secret.

I freshened up and joined John in the backyard, a sprawling area of mostly dirt—nothing ever seemed to grow there—but with a gorgeous view. John had made it more inviting four years ago by building a covered porch with enough space for a table and four chairs. The backyard faced west, and we more often than not enjoyed summer and fall evenings watching the sunset.

John was tending to the grill while we talked about the day.

"You and Walt did a fine job with the tables," I said. "The burial and reception went off without a hitch. I'm sure it took a lot of pressure off Mena."

After having discussed the day, our conversation shifted to Moose. And though John had never gotten to know Moose particularly well, he expressed his admiration for Moose's service. John was seventeen during the outbreak of World War I, and he had tried to enlist but was rejected because of his eyesight. He couldn't see a thing unless he was doing his schoolwork. He scrolled through books using a soup can with a magnifying glass taped to the bottom. It wasn't until John was in ninth grade that Doc Morten, who examined eyes and sold glasses, moved to town. When John got his first pair, wire-rimmed with lenses thicker than a stack of quarters, a whole new world opened up to him. That's when he took to fixing cars.

"So you think Moose will do it?" he asked.

"It's hard to tell, but I'm optimistic."

What I was thinking, though I didn't say, was that we really needed to get Vern McSorley on board. Because Vern carried so much sway in town, I had little doubt that if he were to ask Moose to coach the boys, Moose would coach the boys. But Vern, despite our friendship, never did a favor for anyone without expecting something in return, and it usually involved money. I did not want to be beholden to him, so I never seriously entertained the notion of speaking to him about Moose. I was, however, certain that if Moose became coach, Vern, as well as the rest of the town, would support him.

I then took my first bite of ribs.

"Gets better every year," I said.

SHORTLY AFTER DINNER, John went to bed, and I got to work. Despite the taxing day, the adrenaline was flowing, and I knew I was good for several more hours.

I sat at the kitchen table gathering my thoughts as I prepared to draw up plays, something I hadn't done since I was a child. Before I began, I thought about Burl's funeral, about Joseph Francis and my fears for his safety, and about all the brave men who had chosen war over the comforts of home, whose sacrifices were selfless and noble.

I considered John's suggestion that I coach the boys, but then I shook my head and smiled. Then I got to thinking about how I had learned the game. In the beginning, my father would explain the difference between offense and defense. He'd explain the roles of the various positions and taught me what those positions were called. I was nine years old when he began to teach me the nuances of the game. He pointed out the popular Wing-T offense and explained what types of plays could be run from the formation. He explained the differences between zone and man defenses.

By the time I was ten, I could call plays from the stands. My father listened proudly as I'd suggest formations and plays that could be run from them. Sometimes, when I would get a hot dog during the game, I would tear the bun into small pieces, place the bits on the wooden bleachers, and use them to draw up plays. I would explain that if the halfback were to run off the edge just a yard behind the quarterback, a fake pitch would draw the linebacker in, and the quarterback could easily pick up a first down even on third-and-long.

Sometimes the men in the stands would join in on the conversation. They'd ask me what would happen if the defense was prepared for the play and was ready to stuff it behind the line of scrimmage. Easy, I would say. Using the same formation, just hand off to the fullback and watch him dash straight through the line of scrimmage before the defense knew what hit them.

The men would laugh. I could tell it was partly because they thought I was cute, but mostly because they knew I was right. But those days and those men were long gone.

So that night, as I began drawing up plays, I realized in that moment that I was preparing to share something with Moose that I had grown up expecting to share with someone else—my own child. I realized how much it meant to me to pass along to my child what my father had passed along to me. Football, and its joys, was supposed to be my family legacy—at least, that was my dream.

I put my pencil down and began to relive my cherished but brief moments with my only child, a son born prematurely who lived long enough for me to embrace him. But just once. He died in my arms, the arms I then looked down at, the arms that once held him so tightly—when I knew he was slipping away and I could do nothing to prevent it. So that night, I cradled my empty arms to my chest, bowed my head, and whispered: *This is for you.*

And then I got to work. I drew up more than a dozen plays out of the T formation. Although I knew the plays, I was not familiar with the language the coaches had used to name each play, so I came up with my own—a numbering system. A *cross buck* was a 101, *curl* a 110, *hook* a 200, *draw* a 502. I allowed myself to have fun with one name. Because I knew my favorite author had played high school football, I drew up my go-to play and named it the Great Gatsby. The play required two flankers, one on each side. The ball would go to the flanker lined up on the right. He would run hard for ten yards, then make a sharp right turn toward the sideline. At that moment, he would look back at the quarterback, who would pump-fake a pass to him. Expecting the defensive back to bite, the flanker would watch the defender's hips, and once his hips turned—committing to one direction—the flanker would turn left, hightail it at a thirty-five-degree angle, and catch the ball on the fly. The pass would cover thirty yards from the line of scrimmage and leave the flanker with nothing but open field. It was a play designed to score.

Once I had completed my list of plays, I sequenced them for practice. After that, I drew the defensive schemes from the 7-2-2. Once I had my starting lineup set for both offense and defense, I scratched out a depth chart for substitutes. Finally, I put my pencil down and went to bed.

CHAPTER 3

Saturday

I had never been one to sleep in, but after such a long night, I found myself startled and awakened when the telephone rang at 7:00 A.M.

"Miss Tylene, can you talk?" Moose said from the other end of the line. I knew he didn't own a telephone, so I asked, "Where are you?"

"A phone booth outside the Underwood Café," he said. I told him I preferred to meet and talk face-to-face. He said he'd be right over, but I insisted on meeting him at his house. I figured if he was within the comfort of his own home, he might be more likely to agree to coach. I slipped on a dress, asked John to keep his fingers crossed, and jumped into my truck.

I arrived at Moose's house, and he immediately offered me

a cup of coffee. My stomach was churning, but I accepted. We sat on his living room sofa. The room was oddly tidy, a sharp contrast to the day before.

"I haven't slept," Moose said. "Tried a couple times, but couldn't stop thinking about what you said . . . about trusting you."

"Why'd that keep you up?"

"Because I kept asking myself, 'Why *would* I trust you?'"

"Moose, I know what you see when you look at me. A woman. In her forties. A dress. Pearls. Is there anything about this picture that speaks to football? I understand. But let me give you something."

I reached into my handbag, pulled out my play sheets and depth charts, and handed them to him.

"Here, take a look."

He flipped through them for what seemed like hours, and then he looked up at me.

"Where'd you get these?"

"I didn't get much sleep last night, either, Moose."

"You?" he asked, eyebrows shooting up, revealing that he finally realized I knew what I was doing.

"Yes, me, Moose. Me. And like I told you yesterday, I couldn't have done it without a father who spent countless hours teaching me the game despite knowing I'd never play.

"And even though *I* can't play it, I love football, Moose. I love what football gives to the boys, I love what football gives to a school, and I love what football gives to a community. We're in pain, and we might not all know it yet, but we *need* football. And we *need* you."

Moose stood and began pacing.

I waited. At one point, I looked down and closed my eyes. *Our Father, who art in heaven . . .* Shortly before my thoughts reached *amen,* Moose interrupted me.

"You sure do care an awful lot."

"I saw Jimmy and Bobby Ray at the airfield hangar Wednesday. I saw them watch as the body of their football coach was taken from the plane. They're off to war next. Yes, Moose. I do care an awful lot."

Moose looked at me and in an unconvincing fashion said, "I guess I can't say no."

"Well, that's just not good enough."

"What? I just said I'd do it. What else do you want from me?"

"What else do I want from you? Let me tell you, Moose. If you're agreeing to do this because you can't tell me no, well, I can't accept that. You have to want this. You have to tell me you trust me. And you have to mean it, because if you don't, then we're better off just locking the doors to the field house. Now."

I stood up, grabbed my purse, and turned toward the door when I heard Moose whisper from behind me.

"I trust you, Miss Tylene."

Monday

As planned, Moose met me at the field house. When I saw him, I did a double take. He had bathed, was clean-shaven, and had cut his thick, dark hair and combed it so nicely I could even see a dash of Clark Gable. The air about him was a total departure from the Moose I'd once had in my ninth-grade English class. Back then, I'd ask him a question about the material, and his answer was always the same: "Not today." With my quick glance at him that morning, I knew, *today* had at last arrived.

"Eight o'clock sharp," I said as Moose walked into the locker room.

"You can count on me," he said. "I'm nervous, but I'm excited. I barely slept all weekend."

Because Moose had played for the Lions just three years prior, I had very little to show him. He was familiar with the locker room setup, so we walked onto the field.

"The field's clearly in bad shape," I said, "but don't worry about that now. We'll talk about it after practice when you come by my house. Remember, you'll have the field from three o'clock to four thirty, same as when you played, so I'll expect you by five o'clock."

"Yes, ma'am," he said.

I turned to leave when Moose asked softly, "You believe in me, don't you, Miss Tylene?"

I turned back. "Yes, Moose, I do." I then smiled and asked, "By the way, what do you want us to call you?"

Apparently surprised by the question, Moose stumbled over his answer. "What? Wow. Okay. How about Coach? I'd like to go by Coach."

"Then that's it. Good luck with your first practice. I'll see you at my house by five o'clock, Coach."

He smiled and nodded. Again, I started to leave, but this time I sensed his anxiety, so I stopped and turned to him.

"I'll watch practice from my car in the parking lot," I said.

"What? That's not necessary, Miss Tylene."

"Are you saying it wouldn't make you feel better knowing I'm out there watching?" I asked.

"No, no, I'm not saying that at all," he said. He then paused.

"So?" I asked.

"It'll be awful hot out there. You sure you want to do that?"

"I don't want the boys to see me. Might seem like I'm undermining your authority, but I think I can advise you more effectively if I see it for myself."

"I appreciate this, Miss Tylene. I really do."

I headed back to my office. I kept my fingers crossed, but mostly, I prayed.

I WAS CONVINCED Moose, as promised, would spend the day studying the plays I had prepared. It wasn't the knowledge of football that worried me, though. I knew Moose could *play* football, but I had no idea if he could *coach* it. I kept my promise to Moose to observe practice from afar, but when the boys arrived for practice at three o'clock, I was nervous. I parked two spots behind Mr. Redwine's 1937 Ford coupe. Because of the distance, my pickup could not be seen from the field, but I could only see everything clearly between the twenties. Beyond that, I'd have to find a new vantage point and get to it without being spotted by the boys. I surveyed the parking lot so as to plan ahead.

Moose seemed almost oblivious to the boys as they entered the field house. He was on the field, searching for rocks and tossing them to the sidelines. Once the field house door sprang open and the team began to emerge—offense, shirts; defense, skins—Moose had positioned himself just outside, extending his hand to welcome each boy, one by one. The seniors emerged first. I was close enough to hear.

"Who's this?" Charlie said, his fingers mussing Moose's freshly cropped hair. "What happened to Moose? Where's Moose?"

The others laughed. Moose appeared to ignore the ribbing, but even from my vantage point, I could see it bothered him.

Once everyone was outside, Moose gathered the team together and shouted so all could clearly hear him—including me.

"I was just asked by a senior, 'Where's Moose?' Well, let me tell you something—Moose ain't here. Moose played football a few years ago. Went off to war and came home with a limp and a new life. Now, fellas, I'm *Coach*. You better get used to that, because it's the only way you'll play football this season. Got that?"

Everyone was silent. Then someone in the back laughed. Everyone turned around, but it appeared they were not certain who the culprit was. Then another guy laughed. And then another. I jotted down names.

"Moose—I mean, Coach—no disrespect, but we can't just shift gears like that," Jimmy said. "We stand with you, but to us, you're still Moose. Maybe lighten up a little. It's just kind of weird."

I knew what Jimmy was talking about. Just a few years

earlier, Jimmy's big brother, Stanley, was Moose's teammate. Stanley was captain of the football team, and Moose was known as the team cutup. He was known to be lazy and to have had bad practice habits. But everyone in town knew Moose loved football, and on game day, it was clear: No one was more competitive.

Moose seemed to listen to the boys, but it was time to get started, so with his whistle around his neck, play sheets in his right hand, and a pencil in his left, Moose began his first practice.

He shouted out the names of the starters and told them to take their positions at midfield, the only part of the grass that didn't have too many rocks. Everyone complied, yet each moved slowly in the hundred-degree heat.

"Okay, guys, speed it up," Moose shouted as he tried to hurry the team. "We have only nine practices to get ready for Stephenville. We need to get in shape, and we need to learn the plays. Let's hustle."

At that moment, I thought I'd heard a foot-to-gravel sound approaching from behind me. I was leaning against the hood of my truck when I glanced over my left shoulder, but I saw nothing. I turned back and continued to watch practice. At one point, a play extended beyond the twenties, so I dashed to my right, hid behind Mr. Redwine's car, and squatted so as not to be seen. I took the pen from above my right ear and began jotting down notes when the sound of gravel crunching again caught my attention. I knew the boys couldn't see me from the field, but I couldn't hide from others in the parking lot, so I looked back once more but saw no one. It wasn't until I had an eerie feeling I was being watched that I looked back yet again. This time, when I turned around, I saw that I wasn't alone.

Moonshiner, Roger Duenkler's father, was hovering over my right shoulder. I figured he'd been standing behind truck cabins each time I had turned back to mask his approach so I wouldn't see him. I tucked my notes under my left arm.

"Come out to watch Roger?" I asked. I stayed squatted.

"That was the plan," he said, "until I saw you. I've found your behavior much more interesting. So I'm asking myself, 'What's Tylene up to? Why is she hiding out in the parking lot taking notes?' Can't say that I have an answer."

"All good questions, Gil," I said. I then stood up and walked to my truck. Before opening the door, I looked back at him.

"How can you live with yourself?" I said. "Beating up on your own son."

"No business of yours, Tylene."

"When the welfare of one of my students is in jeopardy, Gil, it becomes my business," I said. And then I leaned in close to Gil and said softly, "I'm going to keep an eye on Roger. He comes to school with so much as a scraped knee, and I'm calling the authorities."

Gil laughed.

"Take my advice: Stick to your own business," he said.

I said nothing, but I was hoping he would do the same.

Gil walked off and headed for the bleachers, joining a smattering of curious onlookers. I stayed in my truck for a few minutes, then got out and got back to work. I took notes while standing beside my truck, the heat beating down on me. I could only imagine how hot it must have been for the boys. Still, I noted: *No excuses.*

About a half dozen boys along the sideline began tossing a football. Initially, I thought they were loosening up, but after a few minutes, I realized that they had plans of their own, and those plans did not include listening to Moose.

"Come on, Moose," I whispered to myself. "Take control."

Instead, Moose continued to engage the starters he was working with. What I could discern from their actions was that the offense was to run a few plays I had drawn up, and the defense was to keep the offense from advancing the ball. It was a walk-through, so there was no tackling, and the boys' lack of enthusiasm left me wondering if they had yet bought in to Moose as the head coach. They continued to go through the motions, but what I was watching was the quietest football practice I had ever seen, and that's never a good sign.

Thirty minutes into practice, Jimmy called the offense, including the reserves, to a huddle. Although I had no idea what Jimmy was telling the boys, I knew he must have said something meaningful, because the remaining sixty minutes of practice were more productive. The boys were slightly more in sync. I couldn't help but notice that Jimmy appeared to have more command of the boys than Moose did.

ONCE HOME, I waited anxiously for Moose to arrive, which he did at five o'clock sharp.

"You clearly learned something in the military about promptness," I told him.

"Yes, ma'am."

Moose entered, and all I could see was defeat in his face.

"What would you prefer, a tall glass of water, iced tea, lemonade?" I asked as we approached the kitchen.

"A tall glass of water sounds great," Moose said. He pulled out a kitchen chair and sat down.

I grabbed a pair of tall glasses from the cupboard and filled them with ice and water. "So, Coach, what's your impression? How'd it go?"

"Not good," Moose said. "I know the boys want to play, but I have to wonder if they really believe we will. Jimmy commanded more respect out there than I did. While I was running things, the boys were slow to get moving, and when they did, it was because Jimmy had taken over. I don't think they take me seriously. I'm sure you noticed."

I put the water glasses on the table and sat directly across from Moose.

"What are you going to do about that?" I asked.

"I was hoping you would tell me."

"You just said they don't take you seriously. If that's true, then why?"

"It's strange. I've seen the boys around town since I returned, and I know they respect me for my service, I really do. They've even said as much. But they don't seem to respect me for *me*. I guess if they honestly thought we'd have a season, they'd work harder, but it feels like they're not convinced. I mean, it's been just one practice, but even to me it felt like wasted time."

"Can you say you took away any positives?" I asked. "What worked?"

"Once we got into our formations, we ran a few plays. The boys seemed to enjoy that. They liked the walk-through, but I felt disorganized."

"That's probably expected for a first day, Moose. Don't beat yourself up over that. But maybe you do need to spend more time preparing. More time looking over the plays. Get yourself so familiar, you can call them without looking at the sheets."

I then reminded Moose that I had already sequenced the plays. All he had to do was have the boys run through them one at a time, until each play ran smoothly. Repetition. Repetition. Repetition. I pounded the word into Moose's brain. *Repetition.*

By the time he had finished his glass of water, I had nothing more to add. Memorize the plays. Know the order for practice. Run a play. Repeat the play. Run the next play. Repeat the next play. Remind the boys of their assignments. Work on technique. Make sure everyone pays attention. Get organized at home; it'll present itself on the field.

"Got that?" I asked. I didn't let him leave until I was comfortable that he was comfortable. I also assured him I'd observe again the next day.

MINUTES AFTER MOOSE left my house, Jimmy arrived. Jimmy told me he had walked the few blocks to my house straight after practice. Said he'd seen Moose's truck outside, so he waited until Moose had left to knock on my door.

Jimmy preferred a glass of lemonade, so once I poured it, we sat together at the kitchen table. From time to time, I'd get up to stir the stew I was preparing for dinner.

"Stanley and Moose were teammates, remember?" Jimmy asked.

I nodded my yes. I knew exactly where this was going.

"It doesn't feel right, Miss Tylene."

"Because it's Moose and not Stanley?"

"When Stanley and Moose played football together, Stanley was the leader, and Moose? I don't have to tell you about Moose."

"I can't fix that, Jimmy. You know that."

In a soft voice, while still looking down at his lemonade, Jimmy said, "It should be Stanley."

After a minute of silence, Jimmy looked up at me.

"This war. It's changed everything. And I'm so angry, I want to just sign up, find those guys who shot off Stanley's leg, and finish the job for him."

I got up to stir the stew again.

"What's keeping you?" I asked.

Jimmy didn't answer.

"Moose is never going to be respected, and you know as well as I do, Miss Tylene, you can't play for a coach you don't respect," he said. "Stanley, he'd get more respect from his wheelchair."

I sat back down, looked into Jimmy's eyes, and asked, "Do you want to play football?"

"I do. I really do," he said without hesitation.

"So?"

"The guys do, too," Jimmy said. "I guess I'm mad at myself for not getting us off to a better start. I need to support Moose. I can't look at Moose and think of Stanley. It's not fair to Moose, and it's not fair to the team."

With the palm of my hand, I tapped Jimmy on his forearm as it rested on the table. I couldn't help but wish there was something I could do to bring Stanley to town to lift Jimmy's spirits and to let him know Stanley would be all right.

"I shouldn't burden you with this," he said as he stood up.

"Maybe I've put the burden on you?"

"Oh, no, Miss Tylene. When Coach Young named me captain last spring, I knew I had to step up. I just didn't have any idea of what that would mean."

"Jimmy, what it means now is no Moose, no season. We'll make this work."

"Looks like we have to, Miss Tylene. We'll make it work. We've got that first practice out of the way, so I guess the toughest part of the season is behind us."

CHAPTER 4

Wednesday

A fter watching yet a third practice from the parking lot, I drove home with more questions than answers. My head was swirling with what I'd viewed as an unsettling contradiction. Initially, I was struck by the boys' promptness and high level of enthusiasm. I was encouraged when I arrived to find the boys dressed for practice and out on the field. They were tossing the football, running routes, punting, and roughhousing the way I'd seen them do when their spirits were high.

Then Moose emerged from the field house, and the team went stale. There was no other way to describe it. *Why?* I wondered. Why did Moose's appearance kill the joy? When Moose called the boys to the huddle, why did they move with no enthusiasm? Why do they appear so eager to play, yet when it came time for an organized practice, they seemed disinterested? I was truly puzzled, and I knew I had to prepare for a long, deep discussion with Moose that night. I needed to get to the core of the problem, because we had to fix it. I was expecting to discuss my frustrations with John when I entered the house through the kitchen. Instead, I found John standing in front of the stove wearing a sport coat.

"Going somewhere?" I asked.

"Yep," he said. Then he smiled. "You're coming, too."

"Going out on a *Wednesday*?"

"Not just out, but out to dinner. *The* dinner."

"What? Why?"

"It's gotten to be like Grand Central Station around here with Moose coming by every night, and now Jimmy, too. Don't get me wrong, I got no trouble with it. But tonight, I want you all to myself, so we're going into hiding."

I laughed. "Hiding?"

"Get your mind off everything. We have a reservation at the Hotel Brownwood steak house. No one will look for us there. Just you and me."

"John, that's so thoughtful, but we don't have that kind of money."

"We do tonight."

Although we rarely spent money frivolously, and we certainly did not have money to spare, I was overjoyed by John's enthusiasm. I felt a spring in my step as I walked to the bedroom to freshen up and change clothes. Like I did every evening when I'd get home from watching practice from the parking lot, I cleaned up first, but instead of throwing on my housedress and slippers, I slipped into my favorite dress—blue velvet that draped to midcalf. I put on a velvet-bowed hairnet with a forehead veil, a rhinestone brooch, white wrist gloves, seamed stockings, and my black peep-toe heels. I also put my short string of pearls back on. I'd never left the house without my pearls, given to me many years ago by my mother.

When I emerged from the bedroom all gussied up, John smiled and extended his left arm for me to hold. Once I did, he paused.

"Just a second," he said, and he walked back to the bedroom. A few minutes later, he returned, only this time without the sport coat. He'd changed into what I'd once told him was my favorite of his two suits, a double-breasted pin-striped gray three-piece, plus a gray fedora.

"You look like a million bucks," he said. He smiled, and with both arms extended from his side, he said, "This is the best I've got." Again, he extended his arm for me to hold. Before we walked out to the garage through the kitchen, I stopped at the front door to tack on a note I'd written while John was changing.

Moose,

John surprised me with dinner out. Let's meet at the field house at eight o'clock in the morning.

                                                    Tylene

"Oh my, John," I said as he escorted me to the car. "We're taking the tin lizzie out tonight?"

I knew that when John took his favorite 1927 Model T out of the garage, we were in for a big night on the town. No expense spared. When I got into the car, John had the radio he'd installed playing Glenn Miller, "In the Mood."

I started to swing my shoulders to the beat of the music.

"I am ready for some dancing," I said.

"I hoped you would be."

"Do you remember the first time we danced together?" I asked John.

"I pray to God I never forget."

It was during my senior year of high school. John didn't have a radio at the shop, but I loved music, so I often sang to myself. I was a little shy of singing in front of others, even John, although by that time we'd been working together almost three years. I'd wait to sing until I was either alone or when the clanging of engine repair work below me had gotten so loud I could sing softly to myself without being heard.

One afternoon, it was so loud in the garage, I didn't hear John's footsteps coming up the spiral staircase. I was singing softly, looking down, working on the books, when at the corner of my eye I spotted John. I looked up at him, and despite feeling red in the face, I'd hoped my volume was low enough to have been drowned out by the mechanics down below. He asked only for an invoice and left. I exhaled and got back to work.

That evening, when the fellas had left and John and I were the only two closing up shop, he called out my name.

"Tylene, I'm coming up," he shouted. I could hear him running up the staircase, his boots so heavy I couldn't understand how I'd failed to hear him earlier in the day. He found me standing, holding my purse, ready to leave.

"What was the name of that song?" he asked.

"Oh, gosh, you heard!"

Then he took my purse from my hand, laid it on my desk, and with his right hand extended, he asked, "May I have this dance?"

I took a deep breath—my futile attempt to alleviate my inhibitions—and I laid my hand in his. He placed his left arm around my waist, and I began to sing softly. We slow-danced in the tiny office space, and I knew in that moment that I'd forever dance only with John.

AT THAT POINT in our drive to the Hotel Brownwood, my frustration had completely dissipated, which I'd figured was John's goal for me all along. As Glenn Miller played softly, we headed downtown in our finest classic automobile. John kept it in pristine shape. It had little mileage despite its age, and it looked as if it were fresh off the assembly line—maybe even better.

As the Hotel Brownwood on East Baker Street became visible from a distance, I thought of how often I'd passed the hotel but how rarely I had looked at it. In fact, it was a marvel—one of the nicest spots in town. Built in 1930 to a cost of $600,000, the rectangular redbrick hotel's twelve stories shot up skyward—Brownwood's version of the Eighth Wonder of the World.

Shortly after the hotel's construction, I joined my father on one of his ranch-related monthly trips to Comanche, a hub for farm resources and supplies. On our return, we'd spotted the building from Early, a small, unincorporated community outside Brownwood, and we talked about how life in the Pecan Bayou was changing. The hotel was the first major change we'd noticed in the area since we'd made our first trek to Comanche for a Brownwood football game in 1911. Comanche was the destination of our first road trip by car— actually, by our ranch's working truck.

I recalled driving down Farm-to-Market Road 1467 with my father at the wheel of an Avery Farm Wagon, essentially a horse-and-buggy but with wheels and a four-cylinder engine. We bounced around, ignoring the toll the drive was taking on our bodies. As we'd travel along the Texas Corn Trail, two hours each way, we talked football, losing all sense of time.

I would bite my nails along the way to the games, always worried about the outcome. On the way back, after having witnessed another Lions victory, I would grouse over having bitten off my nails. My father would laugh.

In 1911, Brownwood played Comanche twice. Brownwood lost 15–0 at home, so when my father and I traveled to Comanche for the rematch, I was, as my dad used to say, a "nervous Nellie." No nerves on the drive home that night, as Brownwood won 17–15 on a last-minute touchdown. Under less unusual circumstances, my father and I would dissect the game on the way back, but on that night, I had lost my voice. While driving home, I slept.

I was so warmed by the memories, as John and I approached the Hotel Brownwood parking lot, I asked him if he could remember the first time he had taken notice of the hotel's visibility from so far away. He couldn't recall.

Having parked the tin lizzie, John ran around the front of the car to my side, opened the door, and grabbed my hand, and together we entered the steak house. Greeted by warm red-velvet walls, gold chandeliers, and waiters in tuxedos, we were set for an evening of elegance—dinner and dancing. The Hotel Brownwood was peaceful and relaxing, unlike a typical Friday or Saturday night when the visiting families of Camp Bowie soldiers stretched the hotel to capacity.

We talked mostly about my mom, school, the auto garage, and how we both looked forward to our upcoming Saturday night of dominoes with Vern and Mavis, something we'd done twice a month for the past several years. When the topic of football came up, John reassured me.

"You have a coach, and the boys are playing," he said. "Certainly, the worst has passed."

Thursday

I waited for Moose to arrive for our daily practice debriefing. I'd seen a particularly troublesome practice for the second day in a row—handoffs were fumbled, interceptions were dropped, snaps were low, frustrations were high—so I expected the meeting to be difficult. Oddly, Moose was late, which made me even more concerned, and when I opened the door, I took one look at him, and I knew it was all over.

His T-shirt was untucked in the back, and he was wearing a pair of old shoes, his right little toe pushing his white sock through a hole. He also had the smell of alcohol on his breath. We skipped the small talk.

"I'm done," he said.

We sat down at the kitchen table. I handed Moose a tall glass of water, and I listened.

"I'm no good at this, Miss Tylene. I wanted to be good at it. I've never been so excited about something in my life. But I go home after our meetings, and I drink until I fall asleep. Sometimes I hear a knock at the door, and I know it'll be Jimmy and Bobby Ray, but I ignore them. I don't want them to see me like that. When I look out the window, I see them walking away, and I can tell they're wondering why I never answer the door. I'm certain they know I'm home."

Moose's hand covered his mouth as he rocked back and forth in his stationary chair. He was fighting back tears.

"I've known since the first practice that I was in over my head. But I really wanted this. I wanted it for me. For you. For the boys. I didn't want to give up. I really didn't. It was the first time I've had meaning in my life since the war. But it's too much for me. I can't do this. I failed you, Miss Tylene. You believed in me, and I failed you."

"Moose, you didn't fail," I said. "The field house would have been padlocked by now if not for you. Every time I watched that door swing open and the players run onto the field, I knew it was because of you. You, Coach Moose Pecorella, kept the boys in uniform."

"Just not long enough," he said.

I wanted to convince Moose to stay, but I could tell by his presence that there was nothing I could do to get him to change his mind. I had come to realize that he *was* in over his head, and it broke my heart.

"What is it, Moose? What's behind this? Why today?" I asked.

"The boys asked how I got injured."

I just looked at him.

"What do I tell them? My buddy gets blown to pieces, and I get sent home? That I'm a fraud? They know I ain't no war hero."

I had known how he'd gotten hurt. The word had long ago spread throughout town, but I asked Moose to tell me his story anyway. I had hoped something in the story would lead to healing.

"What happened, Moose? Tell me."

Moose collected his thoughts for what seemed like minutes, not seconds.

"We hadn't been in the Philippines more than a week. Just a couple days, really. We'd just set up our platoon outside Luzon when we had a little downtime."

Moose then leaned forward, put his right elbow on the kitchen table, and rested his forehead in his right palm. He looked down at the table and stopped talking.

"Then?" I asked.

"We outnumbered the Japanese, but they'd sent their first-line troops. We were a ragtag bunch not ready for what we were up against. Hell, I was in the National Guard."

I moved in closer.

"We were all scared; downtime kept us sane. We had a football stashed away, so I picked it up."

Moose then sat up straight in his chair and started rocking himself again.

"It's okay, Moose. Take your time."

Moose swallowed hard. He looked to be fighting back tears.

"Eldridge Cooper, tall, skinny kid. Scared, too, just like the rest of us. He played high school football, so I called him out. He was still in full uniform, helmet and all, unpacking. I told him to run about twenty yards and cut right. He did, and as he made his cut, I threw the ball. Straight to him. But before he could grab it, he stepped on a booby trap."

Moose's body started to shake and he began to cry. I grabbed his left hand and held it tightly. Moose closed his eyes, keeping them closed as he continued.

"His body. Pieces flying everywhere. I took shrapnel from the booby trap to my hip, Miss Tylene, and I have bits of his helmet—bits of *his* helmet—always with me in my hip, too."

Moose's eyes remained closed, but he could not keep the tears from falling. When he opened his eyes, he looked directly into mine.

"The whiskey keeps me going."

"And nothing else?" I asked.

"I wanted more. I wanted the team to keep me going, but it's too much for me. You've got to know, Miss Tylene, tragedy changes you."

"It does, all right. It changed me."

"You?" Moose asked. "With all due respect, Miss Tylene, I don't think you've seen what I've seen or experienced."

"Your story is tragic, Moose. I can't imagine the horror, and I'm sorry for your loss. But we've all experienced loss. Everyone has. The loss of a child. The loss of a friend. The loss of an entire town."

"A town?" Moose asked.

"Ever hear of the Zephyr tornado?"

"No, ma'am."

"I was in grammar school," I told Moose as I began my story.

My family was living in Zephyr on property settled in the 1800s by my grandfather William McMahan. My bedroom was a converted oversized closet barely large enough for a twin bed. We had a four-room home. I went to bed by seven thirty, shortly after my parents and I had noticed the ominous sky, but it was a common sight for a Texas spring.

I went to sleep with the sound of rain tapping at a tiny window my father had installed when he'd renovated the closet. I was awakened shortly before midnight by the sound of an approaching train. It was a familiar sound, but I'd never heard it at night; we lived far from the tracks. Seconds later, my dad burst through my bedroom door, grabbed me from my bed, wrapped me within the raincoat he was wearing, and dashed toward the backyard underground storm shelter.

My dad held me tightly in his arms as the wind and the hail nearly knocked us to the ground.

"Tylene, you've got to wait for us in here!" he shouted, although my ear was just inches from his mouth. "Wait for me and your mama. It'll be dark in there, but don't be scared."

Despite being pelted by hail the size of quarters, I kept my arms wrapped around my father's neck. His face was bleeding. I didn't know or care if mine was, too. He bent down on both knees and opened the flat-lying wooden shelter door. The wind held it open as he reached down low enough for me to grab on to the rusty metal ladder bolted to the shelter wall. Instead, I squeezed his neck more tightly.

"You've got to let go, Petunia," he shouted. "I'll be right back."

"No, Daddy, no! Don't leave me, Daddy!"

"Grab the ladder! Grab the ladder!" he shouted above the howling wind and crunching sound of rain and ice hitting hard against our skin.

My nightgown was flapping in the wind as I reached down and grabbed on to the ladder. Just as my father let go of me, I saw him lose his balance, falling and smacking his right hip against the shelter door just as it slammed shut.

Barefoot and crying in underground darkness, I kept calling out to my father. My cries got louder each time I'd hear a tree branch snapping or wood peel away from our family's frame home.

Finally, I curled up on the third rung of the ladder. I closed my eyes to keep from staring into the darkness. I cupped my hands over my ears. My shouts turned into whispers.

"Daddy, Mama, Daddy, Mama," I repeated, convincing myself that the sound of their names would shut out the chaos screaming just inches above me.

I waited until all that remained was an eerie silence. I was too afraid to wonder why my parents had never made it to the shelter. I was too afraid to call out their names and get no answer. I tried to push open the shelter door; it was too heavy. I tried again and again. Finally, thanks to a timely gust of wind, I managed to push it up about two inches, and when I did, I saw my father's right boot.

"Daddy!" I shouted. If he responded, I didn't hear. The weight of the door was too much. It slammed down hard. I tried to push it open again, but it wouldn't budge. Over and over, I cried out, "Daddy! Daddy! Daddy!" into the darkness. I got no response.

I began to sob but kept pushing at the door and calling out for my father. Then I noticed a crack of light, enough that only a full moon could provide. The door opened. Standing at the top was my mother, who reached down to help me climb out of the shelter.

"My baby, my baby," my mother said. "Grab my hand."

I grabbed on to her.

"Mama, why didn't you—" Before I could finish my sentence, I saw, just behind my mother, my father's hunched silhouette pushed against a tree. He was barefoot. His clothes were ripped.

"Daddy!" I shouted as I ran to him, ignoring my bare feet while hopping around the debris strewn throughout our yard. When I reached him, I threw my arms around his neck and began to cry. I felt him wince. Then I looked up and saw my mother walking toward us.

I watched as she surveyed the neighborhood under the

moonlight. I glanced around, too, and saw nothing but destruction. Very little remained of our own home. I watched as Mom looked back at the single part of the house left untouched: my parents' bedroom closet. I figured that was the shelter that had saved my mother's life.

"Mom, do you have Frisky?" I asked about my dog.

She did not reply, and I figured she had not heard me.

When she reached my dad and me, she knelt beside Dad. I was on his lap. Mom put her head on Dad's shoulder and began to cry.

Over and over she whispered into his ear, "Thank God you're alive."

Once she pulled herself together, she stood up. "Give me your hand, George."

"It'll take more than your hand, Fannie. I think I busted my hip."

I jumped off his lap. Mom grabbed his left hand, and I grabbed his right. He tried to stand, but he couldn't. By then, we could hear sirens off in the distance.

"My God, Fannie. Look at this," Dad said as he viewed the destruction. I sat back on my father's lap and kept my arms around his neck.

Mom, wearing a nightgown and slippers, sat on the mud beside us and leaned against the tree. I crawled onto my mom's lap, and she began to stroke my hair.

"Frisky is okay, right, Mom?" I asked.

Instead of replying, she hugged me more tightly, and I knew.

The three of us sat there, holding on to each other, until shortly before sunrise.

Two days later, with my father in the Brownwood hospital, the newspaper announced that thirty-five people had been killed and seventy injured. Because the tornado's swath cut through neighborhoods, most people had been sleeping and were unable to react quickly enough to reach shelter.

"You were one of the lucky ones, George," Mom said as she read the paper in the hospital room. Dad shared a room with three other men injured that night. Their families were visitors, too. Everyone exchanged their survival stories, and I realized that not every family had stayed intact. One of my dad's hospital mates had lost his wife. Another had lost two children, including a daughter from my third-grade class.

My father remained in the hospital for months, battling back from his hip fracture and the ensuing infection. Mom and I had moved in with Mom's parents in Brownwood while my dad convalesced. We never returned to Zephyr.

After I had finished telling my story, Moose remained silent. He looked down at his leather shoe, staring at the piece of sock pushing through the hole in his right one.

"The hardships shadow us forever, Moose. How we respond—now, that's what tells us who we are."

"You're right, Miss Tylene. Sometimes in life, we find ourselves in situations we never anticipated, and we end up asking ourselves, 'Why me?'"

Suddenly, I began to sense the tables turning.

"But you know what, Miss Tylene? The boys need to play football, and they can't do it without *you*."

He had me cornered with my own words.

"Clever, Moose," I said.

And then I thought of what John had suggested. Suddenly, I felt a little trapped, a little confused, and a lot of excitement.

Friday

The next morning, I was holding a cup of black coffee in one hand and the newspaper in the other as I walked from the kitchen to the living room and back, thinking about what Moose had suggested, yet dismissing it just the same. John was sitting on his favorite oversized, stuffed chair, reading a magazine and drinking coffee, too. It was a typical weekday morning, except for the decision I had to make.

Because John and I loved mornings, we had always gotten up early, by five thirty; we enjoyed time relaxing together before beginning each workday.

Like I did every morning, I sat on the corner of the sofa, closest to John. I crossed my legs, the sound of nylon hose rubbing leg-to-leg breaking the silence. Then I adjusted my dress so it wouldn't wrinkle above my knees.

"Thousands and thousands of men stationed at Camp Bowie, just a stone's throw from the football field, and *I'm* entertaining the notion of coaching the boys. How crazy is that?" I said.

"Seems to me, if you don't do it, it's over," John said.

Over. Hearing that word reminded me of how much I despised it. *Over.* John knew that word got under my skin, especially when things in life were prematurely *over,* and I knew he'd used the word deliberately. I could have gotten after him for goading me with it, but strangely, I reacted just as I knew he wanted me to.

"Can I do it, John? Honestly, can I do it?"

He put his magazine aside, leaned forward in his chair, rested his forearms on his knees, and looked at me. "Without a doubt."

I got up and started pacing. In the moment, I thought of Moose and how he had reacted to my encouragement in the same way, and I nearly began to laugh. Finally, I told John of my similar conversation with Moose, and John laughed.

"Clearly, you have nothing to be afraid of, Tylene. You know kids. Heck, you were the middle-school English teacher for a few of them back in the day, and they loved you. They know you love football. Did you ever miss any of their middle-school games? They respect you. They listen to you. They admire you. What's the problem?"

"The dress?" I asked.

He chuckled. "And the pearls, Tylene. Don't forget the pearls."

Then he smiled.

"Nothing that we can't handle, Tylene" he said. "You've been preparing for this moment since your father first tossed a football your way. Your father loved you enough to change his life. These boys are your kids. Can you love them enough, too?"

I spent the day thinking of what John said and how Moose had encouraged me, too. I questioned myself, I doubted myself, and I convinced myself that Mr. Redwine would never appoint me as the school's football coach. And still, I couldn't stop mulling over how the boys and the school might react to the mere suggestion.

I paid special attention to how my peers interacted with me. I took note of how Mr. Redwine treated me. I analyzed every interaction I had with the boys.

That night, I told John I had scheduled an eight o'clock morning meeting with Mr. Redwine. I was on the brink of suggesting something crazy.

CHAPTER 5

Saturday

Saturday meetings were rare, but this one had to take place on a Saturday, a day with no phones ringing, no teachers knocking at the door, no students sitting outside the office awaiting disciplinary actions. No, only the two of us.

All I had told Mr. Redwine when I requested the meeting was that Moose had quit, and we needed to talk. I knew he would be blindsided by my suggestion, so I had to be fully prepared. I had to make a case for myself, so I had gotten up early. By four o'clock I had already eaten breakfast and had begun poring over my notes. While I prepared, the only sound I heard was the hum of the light fixture hanging above the kitchen table. Even the birds who sang outside the kitchen window each morning had continued to sleep.

I did not expect Mr. Redwine to ask me what kind of defense I planned to run or what I thought of the single-wing formation, although I was prepared to answer if he chose to ask. I was certain I'd face pedestrian questions, such as "Why do you want to do a man's job? What makes you think you can handle the boys?" And "What does a lady know about football?" I prepared for him to come at me from all sides.

WHEN I ARRIVED at the school ten minutes shy of our eight o'clock meeting, I spotted Mr. Redwine's car in the lot. The side door of the building leading to the principal's office was unlocked. I put my unused key back in my purse, walked in, and headed straight to Mr. Redwine's office, a soft sunlight bouncing off the lockers and the sound of my black one-inch pumps echoing in the empty hallway.

"Morning, Mr. Redwine," I said.

"So why am I here on a Saturday morning?" he asked while he fussed with the coffeepot. "Moose is out. Now what? If you're going to try to convince me that we have time to find a replacement, Tylene, let me tell you something, we don't."

I noticed he hadn't a clue about what to do, so I gently took the pot from him and began making the coffee. Not looking at him as I dipped a spoon into the grinds, I said, "The boys need to play football."

"Give it up, Tylene," he said. He hunched his shoulders as if to say he'd had enough. "We've gone over this. Give me something new. Why did you have to tell me this today?"

"We're running out of time, and I want to do this. Mr. Redwine, let me coach the boys."

84

I wasn't prepared for his response.

"So he was right," Mr. Redwine said.

"Who? Right about what?"

"Gil Duenkler. He stopped by the office yesterday and warned me. Said you'd do exactly this. He called it a coup."

"A coup? Seriously? You believe anything Moonshiner has to say? What else did he tell you—that he's been following me? Saw me taking notes in the parking lot?"

"Notes that he says undermined Moose."

I was livid. I'd known Moonshiner had spied me in the parking lot, but he must have zeroed in on my notes when he'd stood over my shoulder. I had tucked them away from his view, but apparently not in time.

"'Boys don't pay attention,'" Mr. Redwine recited. "'Jimmy needs to learn to pass and not throw.' 'Receivers don't watch the ball into their hands.' 'Backups not engaged.' What was that? A list of grievances to get rid of him? Make it look like you hired him knowing he wasn't capable so that you could step in at the eleventh hour and force our hand? Is that it, Tylene?"

"I'm speechless," I said.

"Don't do this to me!" Mr. Redwine formed a fist with his right hand and extended his pointer finger, pounding it twice on the table and nearly knocking the coffeepot over. "Tylene, you know I respect you. You're a fine teacher and administrator. And frankly, there's no one else I'd rather have in charge of academics. You're the best in town. No question. But Tylene, this is 1944, not 1984. Women might coach football in the future, but they do *not* coach football now! Not even in a time of war. And they *never* do a man's job unless a man is not available. Get Moose back, Tylene, or drop it."

"Mr. Redwine, I wasn't undermining Moose," I said. I maintained my composure. "I was helping him. I kept notes of what was going wrong, and after each practice we'd meet at my house. I'd let him know what I saw and how things could be improved. Yes, I kept notes. Lots of notes."

I turned toward the coffeepot and stared at it while I waited for the water to warm up. The room had fallen silent but for the humming of the machine.

In the silence, my mind harkened back to the day that put me on the path to this moment with Mr. Redwine.

"What was it like for you on that December morning?" I asked.

When Mr. Redwine did not answer, I turned back and saw him looking at me as if I weren't there. I waited.

"Tell me. What were you doing when you heard?" Again, I waited.

"Just come home from lunch, the Mrs. and me," he said. "Mit met us at church and took us out to grab a bite afterward.

"Had the radio going. Angie likes to listen to music after church. Keeps her uplifted. Then, just like it must have been for nearly everyone in town—heck, everyone coast to coast—a live report interrupted the music. I turned up the radio and called her into the living room. We sat on the sofa listening to the reports.

"It didn't seem real until she began to cry, and we both knew that life in America would never be the same—not the way it had been when we'd gone to bed the night before. I guess that darkness was like a curtain. Pulled back that morning, and everything we'd known was gone."

"You did know Jack McSorley was stationed there, right?" I asked.

"I did."

In that moment, I sensed that Mr. Redwine finally understood what it meant, even to him, to keep the boys playing, to keep them home for one more year.

"Tylene, I get it," he said. "But I'm not the problem. So I give you the okay, what then? Have you really thought this through? You're trying to protect those boys, and that's mighty fine, Tylene, mighty fine, but I'm trying to protect *you*."

"I *have* thought it through, Mr. Redwine," I said. "And I appreciate your protection, but I'm not facing war. I can handle myself. You know what else? I can handle those boys, too. And I can coach football.

"Look, if Jimmy had flipped the football to the halfback on the triple option on third down on the last possession against Abilene last season, knowing the linebacker had already bitten on the fullback dive, we would have won the game. If we had stuffed the box, and our middle linebacker had stunted on Abilene's last touchdown, we would not only have stopped the run, we would have sacked the quarterback. Our punt return team can't find the lanes, and our blockers need to improve their torques."

Mr. Redwine didn't say a word. He stood motionless as if paralyzed by fear. Then he began to pace with his eyes fixed on the floor. He ran his fingers through his hair, looked up at me, and appeared prepared to speak, but he stopped himself. He began to pace again, not looking up at me this time. Finally, he took a loud, deep breath, and then exhaled. He turned to me.

"Dagblastit, Tylene."

I waited. He paced some more. He was taking so long I nearly broke the silence, but I waited. Finally, he spoke.

"I can't believe I'm about to do this," he said. As if he were afraid of what he was about to say, he stopped once more and again began to pace.

"What time will you need the field?" he asked.

I smiled, extended my right hand, and said, "The usual—three o'clock to four thirty, Monday through Thursday." As we shook hands, I asked, "So why the change of heart?"

"Because I have no idea what in Sam Hill you just said." He paused, and under his breath he whispered, "Can't wait for Moonshiner, not to mention the Winslow brothers, to get wind of this."

Everyone in town knew the Winslow brothers. All three attended Brownwood High. The oldest, Mac, going on twenty, dropped out of high school after the tenth grade to rodeo in San Angelo full-time. A hip injury set him back, and he returned home. The army wouldn't take him—injury aside, he was classified 4-F, thought to be neurotic and not fit to serve—so when he discovered work was scarce, and there was nothing much to do about town, he went back to high school. His two younger brothers, Tom, seventeen, and Sam, sixteen, somehow ended up in the same grade. I was fairly certain Sam started first grade at the age of five. Now, the three brothers were all seniors, and none had ever played football. Too structured, they'd say. Instead, they were known to entertain themselves by looking for—if not starting—trouble. Often, their favorite targets were their own classmates. And now those classmates would be playing for a lady.

I looked at Mr. Redwine. "Are you afraid of the Winslow brothers?"

"Look, Tylene, my foolhardy decision doesn't mean it's going to be easy on you. Moonshiner, the Winslow brothers, and who knows who else will all be coming out of the woodwork. They will be *pouring* out of the woodwork. Friends will turn on you, Tylene. Honestly, I don't get why you'd want to do this."

"Mr. Redwine, you know it's about the boys. And the seniors? We can't send them off to war before their time. Anyone who can't see that, well, I have no reason to pay them any mind."

I then poured Mr. Redwine his coffee and handed it to him. He sat down, and in a barely audible whisper he said, "Godspeed."

In an effort to lighten the mood before I left, I turned to him and said, "By the way, the O'Keefe & Merritt range in the home economics classroom needs repair."

Mr. Redwine leaned back in his chair and sighed.

ALTHOUGH I HAD preferred to meet with the boys before word of my coaching hit the town, John and I knew something like this would never stay quiet. It wouldn't have surprised me if Moonshiner had followed me to Mr. Redwine's office and listened at his door, just to nose into whatever I may have wanted to discuss on a Saturday morning. In any case, John and I knew it wouldn't be long before word reached every corner of Brownwood. And because I figured the news might not be well received, we considered looking for a café off the beaten path for our Saturday night out—so as not to have to face the public until I'd spoken to the boys. We decided against it. We chose to eat at the Underwood Café. Best not to run from those we'd eventually have to face.

"So, Miss Tylene, Ma Ferguson have to look over her shoulder now?" asked a longtime acquaintance, referring to Texas's first female governor who had held office nearly twenty years earlier.

"No, Mr. Briley, it's all about the boys," I replied as I wiped my fingers on my napkin. "Will you be out supporting the team Friday?"

"Oh, yes, Miss Tylene, you bet. Me and the Mrs. will be out there like we have been every football Friday night." He then leaned in toward me and said in a soft whisper, "Don't you think you got in a bit over your head?"

I leaned back slightly, away from his face so uncomfortably close to mine. "I guess we'll just have to wait and see now, won't we?"

Mr. Briley stood up straight, smiled, and nodded his head as if to say goodbye, but instead only said, "John, Miss Tylene," and continued on to his seat. His wife, Naddy Marie, looked uncomfortable with the exchange but said nothing.

I stared down at my plate, trying not to look around, but I figured John and I were surrounded by the usual Saturday-night crowd—a cordial group, typical of Brownwood. Seldom did the town engage in dissent, and when it did—over things like municipal price hikes, water rights, or school board members—Vern McSorley would step in, make his voice heard, and put an end to the controversy. Figuring I would have our dear friend Vern in my corner gave me comfort.

Not a minute later, I was interrupted once again.

"Can't say I support this, Tylene. No offense."

"None taken, Howard," I said.

John, who had promised me he would not interfere, sat silently.

As Howard walked off, I turned to John. "Will you pass the pepper, please?" I asked.

John picked up the pepper shaker, looked at it, held on to it for a moment, and then passed it to me. His silence told me he was contemplating a tough road ahead.

BY SEVEN THIRTY, John and I had returned from dinner, and we were prepared to host Vern and Mavis for our twice-monthly game of dominoes. Those Saturday nights with the McSorleys had become a tradition, and we eagerly anticipated and enjoyed each gathering. Usually the evening was lighthearted and relaxing, but that night I could tell something was different. We sat around the dining table playing as usual, but silent tension—made more noticeable by rare and superficial conversation—filled the room.

"Hasn't been too hot lately," Vern said.

John replied with a simple "Yep."

More silence.

Finally, halfway through a game, Vern cut to the chase.

"So, Tylene, is it true what I've been hearing around town?" he asked.

I didn't like his tone. "Yes, Vern, it's true."

"Ah, come on," he said. Then he muttered, "Ridiculous."

"Excuse me?" I asked.

"I'm sorry," Mavis said as she turned toward me. "Vern promised not to mention it."

Vern mumbled under his breath something I couldn't make out. We continued playing, but clearly the mood, already noticeably tense, had taken on an even more unpleasant feel.

"I've heard a rumor that the government has an excess of rubber now and the tire ration might be lifted," Vern said, prompting another superficial conversation. After all, we were well aware of the earlier rubber shortage. Until 1943, roughly 90 percent of the country's rubber supply had been depleted, after the Japanese conquered heavy rubber-producing territories like Malaya and the Dutch East Indies a couple years earlier. Those of us outside the trucking industry, and without travel being an economic priority, had driven on dangerously threadbare tires. We all had to make do with what we had before the war broke out.

"Ours had gotten awfully thin," John said.

The topic died, and we returned to silence. Our game strategies were off, and I knew we all had lost our focus.

I thought it might be best if we called it a night, but instead of wrapping up the evening, Vern once again called out John.

"John, what are you going to do about this?" Vern asked.

"Me?" John asked. "I plan on cheering on the boys and supporting my wife. Why would I do anything else?"

"So you're going to let her do this?" Vern said. "You know how bad that'll make you look? I mean, what kind of a man allows his wife to coach football? Not to mention the toll it'll take on you. Someone's got to wear the dress in the house. So what's your color, John? Soft pink?" Vern laughed.

"Please, Vern," Mavis said. "John, Tylene, I'm so—"

"I've been doing some thinking," Vern interrupted her before she could finish. Then he bit down on his cigar. "This whole thing puts me in a predicament. I know you need my fleet, but if I keep sending work your way, it'll look like I support this nonsense. I know work has been slow for you, but I've got to think about my business, and it'll hurt my operations if I have any association with such foolishness. It's just smart business."

I couldn't believe what I was hearing. Our longtime friend, owner of a ten-truck fleet that shipped milk throughout Texas, was about to pull the rug out from under John because he didn't like the idea of me coaching? And it's just "business"?

"Vern, no one else in town can maintain the trucks as well as we do," John said. "And half the other quality shops have already gone under. You can't be serious."

"Damn straight, I'm serious. This is nonsense, and your plan is to stand by and support your wife? What does that mean, anyway? And what kind of a man does that make you?"

"What kind of a friend does this make *you*?" I asked.

"As I said, it's just business," Vern said, looking into my eyes.

The men stood up, walked away from the playing table, and continued arguing. For a moment, I was afraid they might begin throwing punches. Mavis and I looked at each other, and I could tell she was as stunned as I was by the turn of events.

"John, let me tell you something about wives," Vern said.

"No, let me tell *you* something," John shouted. "I know my wife doesn't fit some *mold* you may be comfortable with, but I got no trouble with any of this. She's putting herself on the line for those boys, and I like it. I got no need for you or for your business, so just get the hell out of my house!"

Trying to defuse the situation, I walked over to John.

"John," I said softly, "let's just sit down and talk rationally about this."

John looked at me.

"Tylene, there's nothing to discuss," he said. "I don't want his business." He then stood beside me with his arm around my shoulders.

Vern and Mavis picked up their belongings and headed for the door.

"You're a damn fool," Vern said, pointing his fedora at John while holding open the living room screen door for Mavis. "A damn fool!"

Sunday

John and I had read the morning paper before we made our way along Main Street to attend church services at the downtown First Baptist. The roadside newsie, who shouted, "Lady to coach the Lions! Read all about it!" was nearly out of papers.

"Must feel like Christmas at the *Bulletin*," John said. "Appears they're making a small fortune on newspaper sales today."

I laughed, but it defied my mood. Mr. Redwine and I had yet to make the official announcement, so I was certain our two automobiles had been spotted parked at the school Saturday morning, and gossip spread to a mole who had taken the story to the newspaper. I considered Moonshiner, but Mac Winslow made more sense. I knew that during Mac's rodeo stint he had developed a friendship with a local reporter. Mac was always looking for trouble, and I figured this story, if not handled properly, was certain to create plenty of it.

We made our way to our seats in the large four-hundred-seat redbrick church. I felt the eyes of everyone on me, yet when I'd turn to make eye contact, everyone turned away.

I had convinced myself that if the congregation had turned against me, certainly all fifteen thousand people in town must have as well. But what I found most awkward in that moment was sitting next to Vern and Mavis, whom we'd sat beside in church for at least the past fifteen years. To sit elsewhere would spark the worst kind of gossip; after all, if our best friends had turned on us, why would anyone else care about loyalty? Still, I was not angry with Mavis, and I figured John and Vern would patch things up before sunset. We sat next to them as we always had, but I came to find out I was wrong. Vern was unrelenting.

Once the preacher began, I relaxed. The theme for the day was Samuel 1:17: "Life is too short to allow fear to stop you from your destiny," the preacher said.

Destiny.

I was about five years old, playing in the backyard of our old Zephyr home, when I first heard the word. It was spoken by my father: "Embrace your destiny, Tylene."

Those words might have been forgotten long ago had it not been a typical day changed on its head when I saw my mother crying. My father and I were standing just beyond the back porch on a stretch of grass near the clothesline. He had positioned me about three feet from him so he could toss a football to me. He had me rest my elbows on my sides with my arms extended forward and my palms facing the sky. My father would then flip the football, its tips pointing outward, into my arms. Each time, I'd clutch it as tightly as I had a tiny stray mutt—black, with a trace of Scottish terrier—I'd found a month earlier on our property and asked Mom if we could keep him.

That evening had been unusually pleasant for a Texas summer, perhaps in the mideighties. At one point, I asked my father if I could play football as we had a few days earlier, and not just toss the football. He reminded me of my end-zone destination, and then he tossed the ball into my waiting arms and watched as I'd dash away from him, headed for a touchdown. I could hear my new little dog scampering behind me, and I was certain that if I slowed down, Frisky would tackle me, just not as Dad had days earlier when he'd grab me and circle the air with me in his arms.

"She's to the twenty, fifteen, ten, five . . . touchdown!" His voice became louder as I'd close in on the end zone marked by the clothesline, which we also used as our crossbar—although I didn't start kicking field goals until I was about eight.

It seemed a typical evening until my mother came to call us to supper. I looked up at the sound of her voice and saw that she had been crying. She turned quickly and returned to the kitchen. I can still hear the sound of the screen door slamming behind her. She had never before let it slam. She'd scold me when I would do that. I ran to my father.

"Why is Mom crying?" I asked. I'd never seen my mother cry. I was scared. "What's wrong, Daddy? Why is Mom sad?"

My dad smiled, and he answered me so quickly, I had no time to wonder why he'd smile while knowing Mom was crying.

"Ever hear of happy tears?" he asked me.

"Happy tears?"

"Yes, Petunia, sometimes when people are so happy, they cry."

I was confused. Happy tears? What happened that brought on her so-called happy tears? My father handed me the football and together we walked up to the porch, Frisky trailing us.

"Wait here," he said to me. He walked into the house and returned to the porch in a matter of seconds.

"Sit down, Petunia," he said. He pulled up a chair and scooted it up close so the two of us were face-to-face.

"You're a big girl now, Tylene, so your mom and I agree it's time to explain her happy tears."

I listened intently.

"Your mother and I were afraid you might never walk, and especially never run," he said.

I was horrified, and apparently, he could see it in my eyes.

"Probably not the best way to begin," he said. "Let me start over."

My father went on to tell me that he and Mom first began to notice a deformation in my legs while I was still an infant. It had become most pronounced in my early toddler years. They were so scared, they took me to Fort Worth to see a specialist.

"A pediatrician," my father said. "He gave us the diagnosis. Something called *rickets*. It affects the bones—makes them soft, if they're not taken care of. But there was a cure."

Sunshine. The same light that gave life to our favorite flowers—our petunias.

"Bessie Lee was born with strong bones," he said of my sister, who was seventeen years old at the time and in the house helping Mom with supper. "She wasn't premature, born early like you were. So she's fine *inside*. But you, Petunia, you're our *outside* girl."

Outside girl. I had a role and a reason for it, so over the years, I grew more determined to be as good an outside girl as Bessie Lee had been an inside girl. Bessie Lee could cook, sew, knit, crochet, and keep a house fit for royalty. Although I eventually learned the basics of all five of those things, my burning desire at an early age was to become proficient—a specialist—in everything *outside,* especially football and baseball, my two favorites and the lures my father had used to keep me in the sunshine.

In my mind, I replayed with heightened emotion the words of the preacher: "Life is too short to allow fear to stop you from your destiny." Those words gave me great strength.

Unfortunately, soon thereafter, John and I were reminded that not everyone in town had heard what the preacher had to say—or, if some perhaps did, they didn't care. While the gas attendant filled up our car a block from the church, I heard a male voice from a passing car shout, "Hey, lady! Stay the hell away from football!" I never looked up.

THAT NIGHT, I let the comment get to me, and I finally had to admit to myself that I was scared, but I knew I couldn't let it show. I didn't share my insecurities with John, because I didn't want to bring fear into our household conversation. Plus, with the way things had turned with Mavis and Vern, I knew he was preparing for the loss of Vern's business. So I lay awake in bed for hours, second-guessing myself. Jimmy had agreed to meet me at the field house in the morning, but how was Jimmy feeling about a lady coach? Had I put the boys in a situation even worse than not playing? Would they respect me, or mock me behind my back? I'd built a career as an educator. Would this undermine everything I had worked for? Would I still be an effective administrator if I was a failure on the sideline? My mind wouldn't stop. I tried to block it out. I even tried to replace my thoughts with one of my favorite Andrews Sisters songs, "Bei Mir Bist du Schön," but I never made it to the chorus. I was consumed.

CHAPTER 6

Monday

Rain had stopped falling by seven o'clock. The temperature had dropped, but the humidity had risen. It left for a muggy morning, though it was probably no hotter than eighty degrees. I walked out to the field—eerily empty and quiet at that early morning hour—to meet with Jimmy well before the 8:00 A.M. school bell. Our objective was to put in place a plan to get the field in shape for the season opener, just days away. We also planned to make a list of fathers who might be willing to arrive at the school by daybreak Thursday to get the grass cut and the field chalked.

"Morning, Miss Tylene," Jimmy said as he walked toward me. I had butterflies in my stomach, and I instinctively began to analyze his tone and his movements. Was he comfortable? Was he hesitant? Did I detect any regret in his presence?

My inner fears dissipated quickly, most likely because I had noticed no hesitation in Jimmy. There was no time to focus on any inner fears or insecurities I may have been harboring. There was work to be done.

We walked along a field of weed patches, dirt spots, rocks, and some tall, dead grass that had not yet been removed from the turf. The only area fit for playing was between the twenties, a sixty-yard stretch Moose and Wendell had cleared a week earlier. Although Moose had taken the team through a few practices, it was evident that Mr. Redwine had yet to believe the season would actually be played. During the short time that Moose served as head coach, Mr. Redwine had given Wendell a list of facility priorities, and the football field had not made the list.

"Looks like the team will be busy this week before putting on the pads," I said. Jimmy nodded. We jotted notes as we walked the field together, devising a plan for the team and some local volunteers to get the field in shape by Friday night. As we concluded our observations, I turned to Jimmy.

"Are you okay with this?" I asked. I knew Jimmy would catch on to what I was asking.

"Miss Tylene, Stanley says you know football as well as any coach. He told me that the two of you liked to talk football in the lunch line. He was pretty impressed."

"But are *you* okay?" I asked again.

"Please, Miss Tylene." I sensed he had no intention of expressing any potential reservations. "I respect you, and I want to play football."

I understood what he was trying *not* to say. It had to be

difficult for a boy going into his senior season to be suddenly coached by a woman. How could he know what to expect? I wrapped things up by telling Jimmy that I was pleased to have him serve as team captain.

I left the field confident that we had a satisfactory plan in place and that the field would be ready for kickoff, just four days away, but I was still out of sorts by the time I reached my office. As much as I had tried to put the taunting from the previous afternoon behind me, as well as Jimmy's apparent reluctance to level with me, I found it difficult to focus on my administrative responsibilities. I was certain my conflicted emotions were not outwardly apparent until Mr. Redwine called me into his office shortly before lunch.

"Go home, Tylene. Take the remainder of the day off," he said.

I assured him that I was fine, but he insisted.

"Look, Tylene, once I signed off on this, I signed off on any and all of my personal reservations. But I do know this: You need the rest. Besides, you mentioned earlier that your parents are getting back to town this afternoon."

My parents had been in Corpus Christi visiting Bessie Lee and her family but decided to cut their two-month trip a week short to attend the game. Bessie Lee was accompanying them on the ride back and planned to stay in town for a few days. Her two sons were grown and on their own, but her youngest and only daughter still lived at home, and she promised to give her father three square meals a day and to keep the home tidy while Bessie Lee was away. I was looking forward to seeing Bessie Lee for the first time since she and her husband had come out for Thanksgiving two years earlier. And I was thrilled that our parents would be home to share the experience with me. Their train was scheduled to roll in at two o'clock.

I took Mr. Redwine up on his offer and left school. But instead of going home to eat and rest, I made a beeline for the Brownwood Public Library.

For a week, I'd wanted to prospect the newspaper archives, and finally, I had a couple of free hours to do some research. I found a quiet corner with a large rectangular table near the archives. I set down my purse, a pen, and a notepad and headed for the files.

Once I found the September editions of the *Stephenville Empire-Tribune,* I searched for the Sunday issues. Typically, every Texas town large enough to have both a newspaper and a high school was known to publish a full-page football preview. It didn't take long for me to find the preview. It had been published just a day earlier. The feature photo was of one player: Harold "Red" McNeil. The headline read "Unstoppable." Beneath his photo, it said, "Lucky to have this Irish." The black-and-white picture had the diminutive but speedy halfback posing with the football tucked in his right hand, pressed against his chest, and his left arm extended as if preparing to stiff-arm an opponent. He was in full uniform and leather helmet. His full-freckled face surrounded a scowl and pursed lips.

I copied the names of all team members printed on the roster. Beside their names, I listed their positions, heights, and weights. After reading about the team's expectations, I next went in search of the previous year's preview, which I had little trouble finding.

The 1943 preview photo featured the senior quarterback who led Stephenville for three seasons. He had since graduated and was set to play for the Texas Aggies.

I kept the preview on the table and went back to the archives to find the 1943 Saturday sections—the news stories of the games played the previous nights. Beside each player's name, I listed the stats from each game and made note of game-story descriptions. I pored through the entire season.

Jeffrey Milton, defensive back, 5'10", 160 pounds: Ball hawk. An interception vs. Abilene.

Michael Milton (twin brother), wide receiver, 5'10", 163 pounds: 2 catches-17 yards vs. Comanche. Soft hands. Solid route runner.

Harold "Red" McNeil, running back, 5'9", 165 pounds: 22 carries-115 yards. 5+ yards/carry.

I put a couple stars beside Harold's name. He was the player to prepare for.

I was so engrossed in the research that I nearly lost track of time. Fortunately, the corner of my eye caught the wall clock, and I looked at my wristwatch for confirmation. I was cutting it close. I began to gather the material to return to the archives when, in an unexpected flash, I noticed an announcement about a Stephenville piano recital. I thought I had recognized the name, but in my haste, I had already closed up the paper. For confirmation, I began frantically thumbing through the pages, searching for the announcement. And there it was, the name I had moments earlier scratched out on my sheet of paper: Stephenville quarterback Mitch Mitchell. The article announced that he, among others, was scheduled to play in a piano recital that fall.

Stunned by my good fortune, I left for the train station.

"SHOULD ARRIVE IN about seven minutes," the railroad station's desk clerk told me. With those words, my excitement grew. For the past several years, my parents had been spending close to two months with Bessie Lee's family every summer, and I missed them. I also missed Bessie Lee. We were never close as children, being that she is twelve years older than I am and was married and out of the house before I turned six. Our relationship developed as adults, and even then, we'd see each other no more than once every two or three years. But I've always admired my sister, and I've treasured every moment we spend together.

Once I heard the whistle of a train approaching. I dashed onto the platform. Although I knew it would take my family some time to exit the train—being that my parents were up in years and my mother was slowed by health issues—I couldn't contain my enthusiasm. I stretched my neck with every disembarking passenger. Finally, I spotted my father. I ran to the train to help.

"Dad, grab on to my arm," I said as I took hold of his

cane. He tightly clutched my right arm, and I guided him slowly down the steps. The exit was narrow, so I stepped down in front of him just enough so he could hang on and I could keep him from falling forward. Once we stepped onto the platform, we hugged.

"I've missed you, Dad," I said with my arms around his shoulders. I looked back and saw Bessie Lee leading Mom down the steps, so I handed Dad his cane and ran to them. Bessie Lee held on to Mom's right arm. I grabbed Mom's left arm and together we helped keep our mother steady as she exited the train.

By the time we had made our way to retrieve the luggage, Mom was exhausted, although Bessie Lee said Mom had slept most of the eight-hour ride. Mom had trembles, and we'd feared, without confirmation, that she had the kind of illness that had taken her mother's life many years before. Neither Bessie Lee nor I would utter the name of the illness, but we both knew what each other had been thinking.

I handed my keys to Bessie Lee and told her to take Mom and wait for us in the car.

"Dad will point out the bags to me," I told her.

Not long after, with the help of a porter, we loaded the luggage into John's jet-black Packard and climbed in. No one had yet mentioned why they had cut short their south Texas trip, until Mom prompted Bessie Lee to fill me in on their train ride's most memorable moment.

"So, Bessie Lee, are you going to tell your sister what happened in the dining car this morning?" Mom asked.

Bessie Lee laughed but remained silent.

"Come on," I said. "What happened in the dining car?"

"Turns out there were several newsmen from south Texas on the train heading up to nose around and cover your game," Bessie Lee said.

"Seriously?" I asked, stunned that anyone from that far away would care.

"Come to find out they're traveling up from Corpus Christi, Kingsville, Victoria, and a couple other places. And they happened to be sitting next to us at breakfast. Of course, they didn't know who we were. Probably hadn't even noticed us. And then we hear them start talking about the game. They made comments about how hilarious it would be to see a lady football coach. They were laughing and talking about how they felt badly for Coach Black and the Stephenville boys.

"So Mom looks at me and says, 'Pay them no mind.' But Dad says, 'Fannie, Bessie Lee is a grown woman.' Yeah, I'm grown all right, but I'm thinking that means *permission*."

"Oh my," I said, and laughed in anticipation of where the story might be heading.

"I get up from my seat and walk over to them, and I interrupt the newsmen and introduce myself. Of course, it means nothing to them until I say, 'I hear y'all have heard of my sister.' They look at me and one of them says, 'Excuse me, but who is your sister?' And I say, 'Tylene Wilson.'"

"You should have seen their faces!" Dad said. "Would have thought they'd just seen the Four Horsemen."

"Imagine that, Tylene, I mention your name, and these newsmen think the world is on the brink of the apocalypse. It was hilarious. So I tell them, 'I think you're in for a surprise. If I were you, I'd keep my yapper shut until I knew what I was talking about.'"

"The wrath of Bessie Lee!" I said. I laughed, but I felt a slight discomfort in my stomach. Were newsmen really coming in from towns as far as Kingsville? Was this a much bigger deal than I had imagined?

"I think you're *nuts,* but honestly, I'm tickled pink," Bessie Lee said. "How many people can say, 'My *sister* is a football coach'?"

"What's it been like?" Dad asked. He was sitting in the front seat holding a newspaper he had picked up at the station. He had not yet glanced at it, and I was hoping he wouldn't, at least not until after I had taken him home.

"It's been fine, Dad," I said. "A little out of the ordinary."

"Do they have any idea how lucky they are to have you?" he asked.

"Oh, I don't worry about those things."

Then I saw my father unfold the newspaper as if opening to the center of a book, and I realized what I *did* worry about was how my father might react to the news. I could feel a nervous tension overcome me, and in that instant, I was reminded of what set my love of football in motion.

It wasn't until I was in my twenties that I discovered my own father had known nothing about football until he and my mother discovered my childhood illness and subsequent need for sunshine. Because I was far too young to work the ranch, my father asked the Fort Worth pediatrician for advice on how to best keep a toddler engaged outside.

"If she were a boy, I'd start her on football. It's never too early to start boys on football in Texas," my father had told me the doctor said. He also said the doctor told him it would be more difficult to keep a girl in the sunshine because "girls don't much like to be outside."

That doctor's attitude irritated my father. "I wasn't asking him if you should go twelve rounds with the Galveston Giant," he said, referring to a budding boxing champion from Texas. "I was asking him how to improve your health. Didn't seem the right time to make distinctions between boys and girls."

He also said that the doctor's distinction between boys and girls made him think of the sons—three delivered stillborn within the twelve years between Bessie Lee and me—he and my mother were still mourning. Had his sons been born with rickets, he told me, "I'd have learned football just to keep them outside, too. Why would it have been different for you? You needed sunshine, and your mother and I needed you."

It was during that conversation with my father that I also discovered how he had come to learn football. With Enrique Montano, his ranch hand and a godsend, taking care of the farm, my father managed to slip away some fall afternoons to meet with local coaches and to watch practices. Many also shared their plays with my father, giving him sketches of how the plays were drawn up and how they'd be executed. He'd even purchased a book on how to coach football. He was a student of the game in every sense of the word, and he passed all that knowledge on to me.

Then I heard the ruffle of the newspaper, and my stomach suddenly ached. The *Bulletin*'s sports editor had watched practice from the stands a day earlier, and I'd read his account that morning. But I wasn't eager for my father to see it, though it was nothing we hadn't anticipated. From the corner of my eye, I looked on as my father read the headline: "Football or Foolhardy?"

I ARRIVED AT the field house shortly after three o'clock, allowing for the boys to have gathered inside to prep for our first meeting and field-cleaning chores. I was overcome with anticipation, eager to get the field cleared and the boys in practice mode. I burned excess energy by pacing outside the field house entrance, practicing my introductory speech while waiting for the boys to emerge, but I couldn't help but notice it was eerily quiet. Several minutes later, I knocked on the field house door. No response. I pounded harder to make sure my knock was heard. Again, no response. I pushed the door open a crack and, without looking in, I shouted out to Jimmy. I got no response. The room was just as quiet, so I flung the door open and found the field house empty. At that moment, all the joy and energy was sucked out of me. I hightailed it to my pickup, digging my heels deeper into the gravel with each angry stomp.

Once there, I grabbed my apron, gloves, and gardening shears and marched back to the field. I found a weed patch at the nearside twenty-yard line. I slipped the apron over my head, tied it in back, pulled the bottom over my knees, and then knelt down and began pulling and shearing. I knew we were going to eventually mow the weeds down, but some were so unsightly, I just wanted them gone.

Once my emotions settled, I began to wonder if I was wasting my time. *If only* I had tried even harder to find a man to coach the boys. Had my attempt to help only hurt?

My thoughts were interrupted when I heard the shout of Mac Winslow from the parking lot.

"Why you leaving, Palmer?" Mac shouted. "Going to make your mommy work alone?"

I heard no response from Jimmy.

Leaving? I figured Jimmy must have stood somewhere behind me, had second thoughts, and left. The exchange I overheard only reinforced my fears. If the captain of the football team was not in support of my coaching, who would be? I fought the temptation to turn back and watch Jimmy walk away. Instead, I got back to business. A few minutes later, it was quiet enough for me to discern that the parking lot had emptied and I was free to work without the threat of hecklers or curiosity seekers.

For the next forty-five minutes, I pulled weeds from the roots, laying the long stems flat on the grass until I had enough to load up a wheelbarrow and haul them off to the dirt track. I'd made two trips with the wheelbarrow before I moved on to clear the end-zone rocks that had ricocheted onto the field from the parking lot. I positioned the wheelbarrow near the small rocks and started flinging the stones into the wheelbarrow. The sound of stones tapping against the steel of the hauler cut through the silence, and for a moment I felt like I was not alone.

Turned out, I wasn't. I began to steer the wheelbarrow up the slight incline to the parking lot. I moved slowly, working at balancing the hauler behind the minimal but added weight of the rocks, when I noticed, off to my right, Jimmy and Bobby Ray approaching. Bobby Ray ran up and took the wheelbarrow from me. Without a word, he pushed it to the parking lot, poured out the rocks, and pushed the wheelbarrow back to the field. I stood and watched, taking a moment of respite. Jimmy had remained a distance away when we made eye contact. He then ran down to the field to join Bobby Ray. Once I made my way to the field, I trekked back to the weeds and returned to pulling and shearing. For the next ninety minutes, Jimmy and Bobby Ray tended to the stones, and I pulled weeds. We didn't speak until I needed the wheelbarrow to haul off the weeds.

"You think I have enough here to fill that thing up?" I asked the boys. They had just returned from dumping stones in the parking lot, so I knew the hauler was empty. Bobby Ray pushed the hauler to me while Jimmy trailed behind. Again, without speaking, we filled the wheelbarrow with the weeds, and as Bobby Ray pushed it to the dirt track, Jimmy turned to me.

"I should have been here sooner," he said to me.

"I got the impression you were," I said.

Jimmy looked at me and his face was flush with embarrassment.

"I need you, Jimmy. You know that."

"With all due respect, Miss Tylene, this is not an easy sell."

"I get that. But at the end of the day, you fellas have to ask yourselves: Do you want to play football?"

I paused, trying to read Jimmy's face. I knew if we ever played poker, this was the face I'd see across the table.

"Will you do me a favor?" I asked. We began walking toward the field house.

Jimmy looked at me, but he didn't answer.

"During lunch tomorrow, pull the boys together. Ask them to give me one day. I know they won't buy in just one day into this, but maybe they'll see something there that will allow them to give me one more day after that. Can you do that . . . for us, Jimmy? We can take it one day at a time."

"Yes, Miss Tylene. I'll do that," he said. "We'll all be here tomorrow. You got my word."

I smiled and nodded. The boys then told me there was no reason for me to stay any longer, that they'd clean up and put things away, so I headed for the parking lot. From a slight distance, I noticed a piece of paper shoved beneath my windshield wiper. I grabbed the paper and unfolded the note. It read: *You don't belong here.* It was unsigned.

EARLIER THAT AFTERNOON, I was reminded that the preseason regional coaches' meeting would commence that evening at seven o'clock in the cafeteria at Early High School, just a stone's throw from Brownwood. I'd known about the meeting for some time, but I had since forgotten. I arrived home and began to whip something up for dinner so as not to be late for the meeting. John arrived home soon after, and we ate quickly.

For the first time in years, we had egg salad sandwiches for dinner, but he said he didn't mind, and I believed him.

While I was washing dishes, John sat at the kitchen table and tried to convince me to let him take me to the meeting. He didn't want me to be late, and he claimed he could get me there quickly.

"I know a couple shortcuts," he said.

I appreciated the offer, but I had no idea how long the meeting would last, and I knew John could spend his time more wisely than waiting for me outside a meeting on a hot and muggy Texas September night.

I made it to the meeting just a couple minutes late, but a few coaches were still milling in, registering at the table and picking up their name tags. It was apparent when I reached the front of the line that Mr. Redwine had not informed the regional coaches' association that I would be the Brownwood High School representative.

"This is a meeting for men only," I was told by the man at the registration desk. I looked at his name tag: Coach Brian Wilcox, Abilene High.

"I was under the impression that it was for football coaches only," I said.

"Yes, ma'am. That's correct."

"I'll be coaching Brownwood High this season." I extended my hand to shake his. "I'm Tylene Wilson." He shook my hand but tepidly, all the while looking around, his face asking: *Is this a joke?*

"I assure you, sir. I'm the coach."

"Who do you open against?" he asked.

"Stephenville."

At that point, Coach Wilcox signaled to a gentleman stand-ing off to the side, encouraging him to approach. He did, and immediately Coach Wilcox whispered to the gentleman, who then walked away. I was asked to move to the side while the two coaches standing in line behind me registered. A short time later, the gentleman returned with Stephenville's coach, Rowdy Black.

"Coach," the gentleman said to Rowdy. "You playing against this lady on Friday night?"

"Brownwood's on our schedule," he said. Rowdy looked at me unapprovingly. He shook his head and walked away. At that point, Coach Wilcox issued me my meeting credential, and I joined a roomful of men—must have been at least three dozen in attendance.

I sat near the front, only to hear some salty language between the gentlemen around me. After I sat, they all got up and moved away. By the time regional chairman and San Angelo coach Homer Milson called the meeting to order, I was surrounded by a halo of empty seats. I let it pass. I was too focused on the chairman's reminders of small rules changes, postgame protocol, and new coach introductions.

"It's with great pleasure that I introduce three new coaches to our region," Coach Milson said. "When I call out your name, please make your way up to the podium."

With the call of each name, the room filled with applause. After the third name was called, all three men stood before the room. I could hear laughter coming from behind me and

I figured the coaches were enjoying my public shun. I paid them no mind. I knew I was there for my boys, for the town of Brownwood. What they thought of me was of no concern. At least, not until I was about to leave.

I noticed Rowdy Black standing near the exit, so I stopped to introduce myself and to thank him for vouching for me at the registration table.

"Coach Black, Tylene Wilson," I said. "I'm looking forward to our game Friday night."

Imposing, with his face lined with wrinkles—but none shaped by a smile—and what I figured was a six-foot, two-inch frame, Coach Black looked at me and laughed. He turned to walk away, glancing at a coach standing nearby, and with a mouthful of chew said, "Hell no." Then he spit into the small tin cup he'd been holding on to all night.

CHAPTER 7

Tuesday

John and I awoke to news splashed across the top of the *Brownwood Bulletin*'s front page.

STEPHENVILLE OFFERS FORFEIT TO BROWNWOOD

Stephenville High School has offered to forfeit its season-opening game at Brownwood rather than have its players compete against a team coached by a lady.

"It's a joke to have my boys play powder-puff after all the work they've put in," Coach Rowdy Black said. "We'd rather take the loss than have to subject our fans and our team to a circus act. With all due respect to Brownwood [High School]'s principal, Ed Redwine, I can't even believe he plans on parading a lady coach out there in a dress and heels. That ain't football, and we'll have nothing to do with it."

Apparently, several Brownwood Lions feel the same way. Senior safety Roger Duenkler said he's all for the forfeit.

"I'd rather win than play," Duenkler said.

The student body shares that sentiment, as three brothers, known on campus as the Winslow brothers, expressed their embarrassment at the thought of cheering for their school team, coached by a lady.

The paper went on to quote Jimmy Palmer as saying he was willing to do what his teammates preferred.

I put the paper down before finishing the story. I'd had enough. A few minutes later, I jumped in my truck to head for work.

As I began backing out of the driveway, I heard John shouting my name. I looked forward and saw him running from the house, straight toward the truck, waving his arms, signaling for me to halt. I stopped and leaned out the window.

"Bessie Lee just called," he said. "Your mother fell."

JOHN JUMPED INTO the truck, and I drove us to my parents' home. When we arrived, Bessie Lee asked John to wait with Dad in the kitchen. She and I walked back to the bedroom, where Mom was lying on her bed. Mom's eyes were closed, and she did not acknowledge us.

"She's asleep, right? Not unconscious?" I asked Bessie Lee.

"She's asleep. I promise, she didn't hit her head. Doc O'Hara is on the way."

Bessie Lee proceeded to tell me that Mom lost her balance when she stood up and tripped over her chair at the kitchen table. She said Mom did not lose consciousness and that she managed to walk to the bed with Bessie Lee's help.

"At first, I thought maybe she had just gotten up too fast and let the blood rush from her head, but she didn't get up *that* fast, so I'm afraid it might be something else. I think the disease might be advancing."

"Had her head been shaking much while she'd been with you?" I asked.

"Seemed more noticeable when she was looking down," Bessie Lee said.

"I didn't notice anything yesterday," I said.

"It's been inconsistent."

Bessie Lee and I went back to the kitchen. Shortly after, Doc O'Hara arrived. He had begun caring for my mother when she first experienced the involuntary tremors about two years earlier. Doc had instructed us to keep an eye on the tremors, and if they worsened, we were to call him immediately. The tremors had been most noticeable with her head and hands.

Doc examined Mom and told us he wanted her admitted to the hospital and kept overnight for testing. He said the hospital had far more equipment than he had available in his office.

"Do you have a hunch?" I asked.

"I do, but let's see what the tests reveal," he said.

"Level with me, Doc. It's advancing, isn't it?"

"Seems so. We'll have to determine how to keep her comfortable."

Even Doc O'Hara couldn't bring himself to utter the words *Parkinson's disease* in our presence.

Bessie Lee said that there was no reason for both of us to take Mom to the hospital. She insisted that she and Dad would be fine, so I assured her that John and I would meet up with all of them later that afternoon. I then took John home and headed to school.

Most of the school day was stressful for me. Between Mom's fall, the threat of a Stephenville cancellation, and the lack of support from my own team, I had little ability to focus. I stayed away from Mr. Redwine's office, though. I didn't want him sending me home again. I had too much work to do, and I was determined to get it all done. As assistant principal, I was tasked with all academic issues, including the updating of curriculum, reviewing textbooks, hiring teachers, evaluating teacher performance, attending district meetings, and scheduling classroom utilization. Fall was always the busiest time of year, but Brownwood High School was known for its exceptional faculty, so I never had to look over anyone's shoulder, for which I was particularly grateful.

I did leave campus during the lunch hour to check on my mom, but I didn't give any explanation for my departure. My mom had always been a private woman, and I was not about to breach that expectation.

Dreading it, but knowing that one day I would have to return, I walked into the hospital for the first time since John and I left without our infant son all those years ago. My grief compounded with each step. At one point, I had to stop and close my eyes, but there was no disguising the smell of my surroundings, so I forged on.

Finally, I found my mother's room, a small single, but so cramped there was space for just one visitor at a time. My father was sitting on a chair at Mom's bedside, so I stood inside the doorframe.

"How's she doing?" I asked my father.

Mom opened her eyes upon hearing me.

"I'm fine. Just tuckered out," Mom said.

"Where's Bessie Lee?"

"She's in the lobby waiting area," Dad said. "We've been taking turns."

I excused myself to find Bessie Lee.

"Is my coaching affecting Mom's health?" I asked her.

"Don't be silly, Tylene. We both know this has been coming on for some time."

"I know," I said. "I just don't want to put any undue stress on her. We both know she's a bit fragile."

"Physically, but not mentally. She's proud of you, Tylene. She bragged about you so much on the ride up, I'd had it up to here," she said, resting her right palm on the top of her head.

We laughed.

"I'm proud of you, too," she said. "Don't put undue stress on yourself. Mom's health has nothing to do with you."

Reassured, I returned to my mother's room.

"May I?" I asked Dad.

He got up, hugged me, and waved his palm upward toward the chair.

"It's all yours," he said. He grabbed his cane and said he'd be with Bessie Lee.

I sat and held on to my mother's left hand while she fell in and out of sleep. I looked down at her hand as it rested in mine, and I zeroed in on a tiny scar just below her fore-finger knuckle. The scar, vertical like her fingers and barely visible, couldn't have been more than a couple centimeters in length. It caught my attention only because I knew it was there, and staring at it took me back to the day she got the scar, something she immediately referred to as her "first sports injury."

I couldn't have been more than ten years old when my father and I were outside tossing a baseball one spring Saturday afternoon. We owned only one baseball mitt—the one my father had used when he was a teenager—and it was well worn. My father insisted I wear the glove when we played catch, so he always caught bare-handed. My mother didn't know much about football, but she loved baseball, my second-favorite sport. I noticed she had stepped out onto the back porch and was watching us play catch, so I shouted to her, asking her to throw with us. She had never done that before, so I was surprised when she decided to join in.

"Here, take the mitt," I said, running up and removing it from my left hand as I approached her. She slipped it on.

"Haven't had one of these on in years," she said.

"In years?" I asked. "You've worn a mitt before?"

She went on to tell me that during physical education class in high school, the girls sometimes joined the boys for a watered-down version of baseball—easy, slow pitches and four strikes per at bat. The school was so small, she said, that the boys needed a few girls in order to field two teams.

I was impressed, and I figured she was ready for her first catch in years. I ran back to my spot and threw the ball to my mother. When I heard the sound of the ball hit the mitt, I couldn't believe I was playing baseball with my mother. The three of us threw for several minutes when I got a hankering to "run the bases."

I told my father to throw to Mom while I attempted to steal third, which I asked her to imagine she was covering. I was halfway to third when my father threw to my mother. She caught the ball and began to lean down to tag me as I slid onto the makeshift base—nothing more than a gathering of dirt—but my boot caught the mitt, knocking it off, and my heel jammed into the back of her left hand. Blood began to pour from a tiny but deep gash. I was mortified and immediately began to cry.

My mother reassured me she'd be fine as she walked up to the house with me trailing closely behind her. As she bandaged her injury, she explained that she had lost her grasp while swinging her arm down to tag me. She insisted that she'd made a tactical error and the injury was no fault of mine.

She healed quickly, but the scar never disappeared.

I smiled as I rubbed the scar. A short while later, Mom was awake and fully alert. We had a nice visit, so I was a bit surprised when I got up to leave and she whispered to me, "I'm scared."

"Mom," I said. "We're all here for you. Bessie Lee will be

at the house tonight with Dad, but I'll be here with you all night. I've already gotten the okay to stay past visiting hours. We're all squared away."

Mom insisted that because there was no room for a roll-away bed, there would be no need for me to stay. It was a tepid protest—I knew she wanted me with her. I told her I would arrive late, but I'd be back. She smiled and closed her eyes.

As I drove to work, I thought of those words I had never before heard my mother utter: *I'm scared.* I was rattled by those words, even though I knew she would be scared. Of course she would be scared. Who wouldn't be scared? But *my* mother? A woman who could snap a chicken by the neck, pluck it, and cook it up for supper? A woman who was as natural with a shotgun as with a skillet? A woman who had survived the 1896 Sherman tornado that killed seventy-five people and the 1909 Zephyr tornado that killed thirty-five?

Still, with each tumble—and there had been three others—the subsequent recovery time extended and her energy level tapered off. On that day, she was weak and frail, and self-ishly I worried that my own memories of my mother's more youthful years would someday fade away.

But they hadn't yet, and I smiled to myself, reflecting on my earliest recollection of the impact she had made in my life—on my first day of school, when my mother walked me, hand in hand, into the classroom and met with my teacher. I was standing to her left, looking up, listening to each word she spoke.

"Tylene is a smart girl," my mother told Mrs. Kennedy.

"I take education very seriously, and she already knows her ABCs. She can read some, too."

I remember how proud I felt listening to my mother boast about me. I also remember how proud I felt while standing beside her, still holding her hand, certain that my classmates had already determined that *I* had the most beautiful mother of all. She was thirty-six years old that day, with her stunning five-foot, seven-inch frame draped in a flower-patterned dress, with eye-catching shoulder-length dark-red wavy hair, rosy cheeks, and naturally fire-red lips.

Before she left, she squatted and looked directly into my eyes.

"Mind your teacher, Tylene. And always remember, learning is fun."

She then stood up and turned to leave. I wanted to cry. I wanted to run after her. I wanted her to stay.

I realized while arriving at the high school two hours late that, other than time, nothing had changed for me. I still wanted my mother to stay—to be healthy and young and happy and strong and beautiful. And I walked to my office still wanting my mother to be proud of me. It was, after all, my mother who had instilled in me the love of learning. Had she not boasted of me to Mrs. Kennedy that day so many years ago, and had she not encouraged me to study hard all along the way, I know I'd never have become a teacher and school administrator. I owed all of that to my mother. The thought forced me to choke back my emotions. But it also made me smile, for in my mind, I had just seen my mother at thirty-six again.

BY MIDAFTERNOON, I was fully immersed in preparations for a curriculum meeting when Jimmy stopped by my office. He had only a couple minutes before his next class, so we talked briefly about the article in the *Brownwood Bulletin*.

"We're going to play, Jimmy," I said.

"No one is as sure of it as you are, but I did manage to convince the fellas to come out this afternoon," he said. "Just a heads-up, though. They may show up more out of curiosity than commitment."

"That's fine with me," I said.

I didn't tell him about the note I'd found on my windshield the evening before. I figured it wouldn't take long for me to determine if it was placed by a football player or not. I naturally suspected Mac Winslow, but I couldn't be sure, so I intended to evaluate the attitude of each player during practice.

I was outside the field house a little before three o'clock, and as each boy entered, I told them to prepare to begin practice with some solid running around the track. Shortly after the last boy entered, Jimmy made his way to me.

"They're complaining, right?" I asked Jimmy.

"It is odd to run laps *before* practice," he said.

"Everything has a purpose," I assured him, but I could see in his face he wasn't convinced. I felt no need to tell him my objective was to evaluate the boys, get a sense of their attitudes. I wanted to know who was on board and who wasn't, and that included Jimmy.

Jimmy waited with me, and as each boy emerged, I shouted, "Get started!"

"This is crazy!" I heard Kevin say as he rounded a corner. I remained quiet, jotting down notes as each ran past me.

Bobby Ray-having a good time
Jake and Kevin-bad attitudes
Jimmy-not yet buying in
Charlie-not trying
Roger-indifferent

After a fifteen-minute run, I called the boys in to midfield. Save for Bobby Ray, all I saw was a blur of collective cynicism.

I knew the first thing I had to do was discuss the article with them and determine if they were in this for the long haul or just in attendance out of respect for Jimmy. I asked the boys to form a circle around me and take a knee. I then looked at each one and asked, "Who would rather win than play?"

No one responded.

"Let me tell you something, fellas," I said. "This is football. Seniors, you're a year away from enlisting. And that will be *war*. Trenches will no longer be the line of scrimmage. Battle will no longer be four quarters. A bomb will no longer be a deep pass. Let *that* sit for a moment. A year from now, you'll see things and do things that today you can't even imagine—because today, you are in *high school*. You have one season. The last season. Do you want it?"

The huddle remained silent.

Then Charlie whispered something under his breath, and I was reminded of why this was not an easy decision for the boys.

"My brother's off fighting a war, and I'll be coached by a lady."

"Y'all catch that?" I asked the team. "Charlie reminded us that while your brothers are fighting a *war*, you'll be coached by a lady. Is that the ultimate indignation?"

I could tell from Charlie's expression that he had not intended for me to hear his remark. Nonetheless, it was best that I did. Was the thought of playing for a woman more reprehensible because of, and not in spite of, the war?

"Miss Tylene," Jake said, "most of us got older brothers off fighting the Nazis, and you're asking me if I'm willing to play football for a lady?"

"Same here, ma'am," Kevin said. "Coach Young, rest his soul, did his duty, and Coach Francis is off doing his. I know I'm still in high school, but where does it say that I gotta play for a lady?"

"Miss Tylene, you know we all want to play football," Jimmy said. "We've looked forward to this season since we were knee-high. But this isn't what we expected. It just doesn't feel . . ." He didn't finish his thought.

"The men are gone," I said in a whisper. "There's nothing I can do about that. Coach Young, Coach Francis, your brothers, some of your fathers. Your turn is coming, but it hasn't come yet. You can play this season the way you've always wanted to or not. You decide."

I paused for at least a couple minutes. Relieved when no one walked away, I began splitting the duties among the squad. I had to keep us moving forward, so I assigned two-way players to work with teammates at their strongest positions. Linemen were assigned to pull weeds, backs and receivers to push mowers, linebackers to haul off rocks. Not long into our field chores, I noticed we'd attracted onlookers: the Winslow brothers, joined by a few friends, none of whom I recognized as Brownwood students.

"I hear a vacuum cleaner works best on a dirty football field!" one yelled from his seat in the stands.

"Are heels the new cleats?" shouted another.

"Do they have football skirts in our school colors?"

At first, I feigned deafness to the taunts, hoping the squad did, too. But as the jeers kept coming, I could no longer fend off my curiosity. I turned and looked at Jimmy. I could see he was furious. I also looked on as Roger started toward the stands, only to be held back by Jimmy and Bobby Ray. I chose to let the boys handle the situation on their own. No sense in giving the Winslow brothers more fodder, but I could hear it all.

"Ain't worth it," Bobby Ray said.

"I don't know if I can take this," Roger said.

"It's not easy on any of us," Jimmy said. "Walk if you want to. No one's got you by the ankle."

With both little fingers extended from his fists, a Winslow brother shouted to Roger, "Come on! You got dukes or pinkies?"

"You have no idea how much I hate this," Roger told Jimmy as he turned back to work on the field.

"Yeah, I kind of do," Jimmy said.

I kind of do? I knew Jimmy needed convincing, but how

deep did his discomfort run? I had to do something immediately, so I gathered the boys together to have them run
through a few plays. I had hoped that playing a few downs of
football might remind them of why they were there.

I stood up, brushed off the dried dirt from my dress, blew
my whistle, and walked toward midfield. I signaled with my
right arm to come on in. "Hustle!" I shouted.

"Hear that boys? Your mama's calling you!" Mac Winslow
yelled.

Fortunately, no one turned his way. I hollered out to Bobby
Ray, asking him to run to the field house and grab a football.
I then split the team up—offense on one side, defense on the
other.

"We're going to run a few plays before getting back to field
cleanup," I said. "Jimmy, take the ball." I handed it to him.
"Line up behind Charlie."

Up and down the line I went, calling out names and as-
signing positions. "Willie, H-back. Jake, left tackle." As I
yelled out each boy's name, they took their positions. Once
I had all starters in place, I began naming backups. In just
minutes, I had everyone in position.

"If you're not a starter, move to the sideline for a few
plays. We're going to rotate assignments. Watch what we do
at your position, and be ready to do it when I call your name.
We'll run the same offense and the same defense you're accustomed to running, but we're going to tweak a little of what
you do. Watch closely. This is a walk-through, so no hitting,
and certainly no tackling."

The boys ran a triple option and Jimmy ran a keeper

around the right end. I had the boys run the play again, only this time, I had Jimmy pitch the ball to Willie. Willie took the pitch and ran hard down the right sideline where at about seven yards downfield, he was sucker punched by Roger. Willie slammed the ball down and went after Roger.

"You trying to kill me?" Willie shouted as he grabbed Roger by the T-shirt. Roger then slugged Willie in the gut, and as Willie hit the turf, his left leg inadvertently kicked the football down onto the track.

"This ain't powder-puff," Roger shouted as he egged Willie on.

The two had begun wrestling on the ground when I caught up to them. Meanwhile, the Winslow brothers had been shouting out instructions as if ringside at a Joe Louis bout.

"Get up! Get up!" I shouted. "You're acting like fools!"

By the time the two boys stood up, they were surrounded by teammates. I walked into the center of the circle, straight to Willie and Roger.

"As long as we have eleven players, we'll play. Many of you are two-way players anyway. So that's all we need. Eleven. And those eleven will play Stephenville on Friday. Now, I've done more than my share of begging just to stand here before you today. I'm done begging. If any one of you has doubts, feel free to leave and take those doubts with you. Frankly, I'm tired of this. I'm here to coach football. We've got three days to get ready. So stay or go. But if you stay, it's time to get serious. Put away your reservations, because they'll only hold us back."

I walked out of the circle and back to midfield.

"Mama's waiting!" Mac shouted.

I didn't look toward the Winslow brothers. Instead, I looked toward the boys. They appeared to be talking among themselves, but I couldn't hear them. Moments later, they joined me.

Again, I had the defense line up on one side and offense on the other. I looked around for the football, and when I spotted it on the track, I saw Moose a few yards off.

"Moose!" I shouted. "Fetch the football!"

Moose limped hastily toward the football, and I could tell by his expression that he knew: I had just named him my assistant. He picked up the football, and before he had taken three steps in my direction, I looked at him and jerked my head back. He nodded, and I knew he understood what I was after, so instead of walking the ball up to me, Moose threw a spiral with the velocity a peregrine falcon would envy. The pass was slightly high, so I leaned to my left, tiptoed, then extended my left arm skyward and caught the ball in the palm of my left hand. I pulled it in and gently cradled it as if holding a sleeping infant. I kept my eyes on the ball from toss to catch to cradle. I then looked up. Eyebrows were raised, jaws were dropped, and not even an eyelash fluttered. The Winslow brothers went mute.

Bobby Ray broke the silence when he turned to Jake and said, "She can throw like that, too."

I didn't react, but I knew I had an ally. Bobby Ray had already admitted to me when we discussed *Little Women* that he had a soft spot for strong women.

"Before the skirmish, I watched you block," I said to the offensive linemen. "And guess what? I didn't like what I saw.

Either you never have learned to block, or you've never cared to block. Regardless, you're going to learn now, and you're going to care.

"So listen closely. Jimmy, Charlie, set up here." I positioned the two boys at the fifty-yard line. I called out the names of the offensive linemen and instructed them to take their positions. I then did the same with the defense.

I stood opposite Charlie.

"Get in a four-point stance," I told him. "Get ready to snap to Jimmy."

I then got into my stance from the noseguard position, opposite Charlie, and shouted, "Hut!" Charlie snapped the ball and I came up on Charlie, torqueing his body to his right. He wasn't resisting, so I had little trouble moving him. But I grabbed hold of his T-shirt right at the neck and held it, making his eyes level with mine.

"Nobody beats you. Got that?" I could tell he was stunned by my tone.

"Yes, ma'am," he said.

I then turned back to the offensive line.

"That's what I want from each of you," I said. "Stop straight-on blocking. Instead, come *up* on your rusher. Torque his body away from the play. Move his hips. Make him adjust. I guarantee it will give Willie an extra half second to hit the hole right up the middle. You'll be amazed at how big a difference a split second means to a play. We need to improve our blocking if we're going to take down Stephenville, right?" I then shouted toward the reserves on the sideline. "Did you catch that, fellas?"

135

"Yes, ma'am!" they shouted.

"Let's do that again," I said. Only this time, I had Charlie line up against Albert, our starting noseguard. I took Jimmy aside.

"The gut will be wide open. Don't hesitate on the handoff. Straight up," I said.

"Yes, ma'am," Jimmy said. But I could tell he was confused by my certainty.

Before the snap, I shouted to Albert. "Looks like you've never lined up against a four-pod, triple-quint option," I said. I made that up.

Albert looked puzzled as he looked up at me.

"If I were you, I'd move about a foot to my left," I said.

Albert moved.

Jimmy called for the snap, handed off to Willie, and we all watched as Willie hit the gaping hole up the middle and ran forty yards into the end zone. I then looked at Charlie.

"It'll work. Once," I said. "Use it."

The boys began laughing. Willie, running back to the line, thumped his chest with his right hand while holding the football up with his left. Albert just looked down and shook his head.

I continued to focus on individual skills while running plays. Occasionally, I would draw up a play in the dirt track, just to remind the boys where they were supposed to be at any given time. It wasn't too difficult, considering the team had run plays from one basic offensive formation. I had the defense split time practicing both zone and man-to-man coverages.

Once I was convinced I had the attention of the boys and that the Winslow brothers were no longer a nuisance, I had the boys return to their field-clearing chores. I went back to my spot with the linemen. I started pulling and softly singing a little ditty.

"'New San Antonio Rose'?" Charlie asked upon recognizing the tune.

"That's right, Charlie," I said. Then I leaned in as if to share a secret with him.

"My college minor was voice," I said.

He smiled, and I sensed we just bonded over something no one else knew.

"How'd you come to know football?" he asked me, prompting the other linemen within close proximity to look on.

I glanced up at Charlie, smiled, then turned back and continued pulling weeds.

"I was a little girl when I first watched a football game. On this field. My father and I rode my favorite horse to the game, and I'm pretty sure I was hooked from the coin toss on."

The boys laughed.

"Seriously," I said. "I borrowed a wooden nickel from my father that night and practiced the coin toss until my mother heard me knock that coin against my bedroom window. She came to my room and caught me flipping the thing midair. She made me go to bed, but it was the first time I fell asleep thinking about football."

I told the boys that I was five years old, and I not only practiced the coin toss, I reenacted nearly everything I had seen. With the flip, I'd whisper, *"Tails!"* Being that I'd win each toss, I'd next whisper, *"Offense."* With my small baby doll doubling as a football, I'd cradle her in my arms and weave from one side of my room to the other. As I'd approach my bed, I'd fall as if having been tackled.

"I was trying to keep quiet so as not to get caught by my parents. It had been well past my bedtime."

They laughed.

I went on to tell the boys about my father-daughter nights and how my father had taught me everything I knew and appreciated about the game.

"There's something special about Texas football," I said. "I truly believe that. I can't tell you how many times I've looked at a Texas sunset only to see a goalpost cut through the yellow and red splashed across the sky. Can't say that I figured I'd coach it someday, but I promise you, boys, I'll give you all I've got."

Finally, practice ended, and once the boys had cleared out of the locker room and only Wendell, Moose, and I remained, the three of us took inventory of first-aid supplies: tape, bandages, rubbing alcohol, liniment, and cotton swabs.

I decided to head to the downtown pharmacy to pick up a few extra supplies and asked Moose to join me. As we drove through the high school's surrounding neighborhood, Moose told me he felt more comfortable working with me rather than leading the team himself. He thanked me for the second chance and promised not to let me down. I believed him.

"You know, I woke up this morning and thought I had nothing to look forward to," he said.

"Now you do."

We made a turn onto Fourth Street, a tree-lined, narrow road of modest wood-sided houses—bicycles in nearly every yard either leaning on the porches or lying flat on the lawn. I was accustomed to seeing the bicycles in the yards, but two caught my eye—army brown with red seats—official military bicycles used for dispatch and messenger services and typically mounted in town only to dispatch devastating news to families. Everyone was known to avoid eye contact with the "soldiers on the bicycles." These bicycles were parked in front of Ida Mae's house.

I knew Ida Mae's husband, Ernie, was out of town. He spent much of the workweek in Midland. He was a roughneck, had been for nearly twenty years. Their son, Nick, had been drafted a year earlier, halfway through his senior year, and I hadn't seen him since.

As Moose and I approached Ida Mae's home, I downshifted, took my foot off the accelerator, and slowed to a crawl.

"I think you need to pull over, Miss Tylene," Moose said, a sense of urgency in his voice. "I'm about to get sick."

As I did, Moose jumped out and ran behind the pickup. I heard him coughing and dry heaving, and then I saw Ida Mae sobbing, sitting on the top step of the walkway leading to her front porch. I pounded the palm of my right hand against the steering wheel, looked up, closed my eyes, and fought back tears. For a moment, I couldn't move. But I knew I had to pull myself together. Moose was physically reacting to news of Nick's death, and he needed me, and I knew I had to get to Ida Mae. I took a few deep breaths, ran my right forefinger beneath my eyes to wipe away my tears, and got out of the truck. First, I checked on Moose.

"Am I looking at Eldridge Cooper's mom?" he asked.

"Deep breaths, Moose. Take deep breaths."

Moose was sweating profusely, and as he rubbed his forehead with his right forearm, he apologized.

"Don't apologize, Moose. I'd expect this kind of reaction. Look, I know Ernie is out of town, so I'm going to check on Ida Mae. I'll bring you a glass of water."

Moose nodded and got back into the truck. He sat inside with the door open.

As I approached, the soldiers, just ahead of me and seemingly unaware of my presence, boarded their bikes and began to ride off. Ida Mae had remained seated on her front step. I walked up, sat beside her, and put my arm around my friend's shoulders. Ida Mae leaned in and rested her head on my shoulder. She startled me when she suddenly stood up and marched into her house. I followed her.

"Look," she said, reaching for a piece of paper resting on the dining table. "A letter from Nick. I got it today. You don't just die the day you mail a letter. It's not possible. Who do I call? How do I get this corrected?"

She started toward the telephone, but stopped and turned toward me.

"Should I write instead?" she asked. "Who do I write to? Or would a call be better?"

"Ida Mae," I said softly.

"He's not dead, Tylene! Where's Ernie? Did you see Ernie?"

"No," I said. "I haven't seen Ernie."

"I need to find Ernie. He has to take me to the Western Union," she said. "I have to go get Nick. He'll be back. His brother came back. He'll come back, too. I know he'll come back!" Ida Mae's voice amplified with each declaration.

Ida Mae kept shouting, "He'll be back!" She spoke so loudly and so often that it eventually wore her down. She collapsed on the couch and began to cry uncontrollably.

"Will he come back, Tylene?" she whispered through sobs.

I sat beside her and rubbed her shoulder.

"He has to come back," she whispered. "He's my baby. My Nick. He has to come back. He has to come home."

I walked to the front porch and signaled for Moose to come up. I then went to grab him a glass of water. He took it and waited for me out on the porch.

I stayed with Ida Mae for about thirty more minutes. I had called her older son, Fred, and I waited for him to arrive before Moose and I left.

As Moose and I headed to the pharmacy, I sensed that Moose preferred to be alone with his thoughts. Only once did he speak up.

"Will she be okay?" he asked.

Instinctively, I wanted to say no. I wanted to tell Moose that I, too, had lost a son, Billy, who didn't live long enough to take more than a handful of breaths from this glorious earthly world. I wanted to tell Moose that from a mother's perspective, there is nothing worse than the loss of a child. That Ida Mae would spend the rest of her life living through Nick's friends—the experiences, the milestones—when they married, when they had children. I wanted to tell Moose that every mother, myself included, would do anything within her power to see to it that the boys her son once knew or would have known would get all the opportunities in life that her son could not. But I did not want Moose to harken back to Eldridge Cooper's mother, so I kept my reply simple.

"In time."

AFTER PICKING UP supplies from the pharmacy, I returned Moose to his pickup at the school, and I stopped by the auto shop to let John know he was on his own for dinner.

"I'll be out late," I told him while sitting in my truck, parked behind an occupied garage.

"What time should I expect you?" he asked.

"Depends on how long it takes me to convince Rowdy Black to stop talking nonsense."

"You're going to Stephenville? Now? It's sixty miles away."

"Looks like I've got to," I said. "He's already dismissed me once. It'd be too easy to dismiss me again, especially over the phone. I've *got* to force him to talk to me."

The sound of the engine hummed.

"Let me take a quick look," John said, and added a little motor oil.

Just before heading off, I handed him written instructions on how to warm up the leftover casserole. I even included instructions on how to turn on the oven. I felt guilty as I left him behind, but soon after, my mind began to wander as I drove along the two-lane dirt road to Stephenville. Occasionally a car heading in the opposite direction would come my way. We'd honk and nod at each other as we passed. But mostly, I saw longhorns. Lots of longhorns. If the wind swirled and I got caught in a gust coming from my northeast path to Stephenville, I was reminded of just how many longhorns there were.

I had the radio going for a bit, and when Ernest Tubb's "Soldier's Last Letter" came on and I heard the words, I became even more resolute.

As I drove through Dublin and passed by the home of the Dr Pepper plant, I thought of how nice it would be if Coach Black had a cold Dr Pepper on hand. But my focus was on my boys, and I knew I had to rein in my anger. The long drive gave me enough time to cool down. By the time I arrived at the Blacks' home, I still had no idea what I was going to say, but I did know this: I was going to speak from the heart.

When Hazel Black answered my knock at her door, she was wearing her apron, and I feared I had interrupted the family's supper. She told me she and her husband had finished their evening meal, and she was simply cleaning up.

Hazel was a tall woman, and I had to crane my neck to speak to her. She had salt-and-pepper hair and big green eyes. She looked either worn down by life in general or by life with Rowdy Black in particular. In either case, Hazel said that Rowdy was sitting out on the back porch, and then she left the room to inform her husband of my unexpected arrival.

I was standing in the living room, close enough to overhear them.

"Rowdy, Tylene Wilson is here, that lady coach from Brownwood," she said.

"Dadgum it, why's *she* here?"

"She said she needs to talk to you."

"I got nothing to say to her."

Then the volume of their voices dropped. I heard some whispering, but I couldn't make out what they were saying. When Hazel returned to the living room, she offered me a seat on one end of the sofa. She sat on the other end. We had little to say to each other, so it was quiet and particularly awkward.

Finally, she spoke. "I helped out some at the plant for nearly a year. Didn't go over well with Rowdy, even though we both knew the help was needed."

I nodded. I figured it was her way of letting me know that her husband didn't believe in a woman doing a man's job even during a time of war. I appreciated her comment.

When it became apparent that Coach Black was in no hurry to meet me, Hazel offered me a Dr Pepper. Shortly after I was handed a frosty mug, Coach Black entered the room. He stood in front of me, but I remained sitting, hoping he would sit, too. Because his size was so imposing, I didn't want him to take on a position of superiority.

"Look, lady—it ain't personal, but you're wasting your time," he said.

I looked up at him and asked, "Tell me then, why do you coach?"

He sat on the sofa, catty-corner to my left.

"I know where you're going with this, and it ain't going to work. Look, lady, this whole thing is strange. It's strange for me, and it's strange for my boys."

"Have you thought about *my* boys?"

"That ain't my job."

"I think it is."

"Look, it's mighty fine you want to help out, that you want to get those boys on the field, but it's flat-out silly, and I want no part of it."

"What bothers you? Playing against a woman, or losing to one?"

"Losing?" He laughed. "That ain't *never* crossed my mind."

"Then what is the problem?"

"There *is* no problem. I just don't want my boys playing against a team coached by a lady. That ain't football."

"So let me see if I've got this straight. Twenty-two boys line up. Eleven versus eleven. Toe to toe. They battle each other for four quarters. They hit, they run, they block. And you think a lady standing on the sideline changes all that?"

"What about the attention?" Coach Black asked. "The place will be a circus. I hear newsmen are coming from San Angelo. Radio fellas, too."

"What's wrong with that?" I asked. "If your team's so good, you'll get an opportunity to showcase it to the whole state."

"It's nothing special when the game's a-whoopin'," he said.

"We'll go easy on you."

That time, Coach Black did not laugh.

"I know you've got a speedy halfback, and most of your defense returned from last season," I continued. "We'll be ready. I don't want to give away my game plan, but if your line splits are too wide, your big boys better have quick feet, because we're stunting. We run a triple option, too, so we've been practicing against *your* offense every day, and I'd put my twenty-two against anyone in the state. I guarantee, by the time the game gets under way, even *you* will forget about the lady on the opposite sideline."

I could tell I'd hit a nerve. Coach Black's eyebrows shot up.

"I need to think about this," he said.

"I'll be in the office tomorrow morning by seven thirty. Call me at home before I leave."

I had grabbed my purse and stood up when Coach Black said, "We'll play. Most dang fool thing I'll ever do, but we could use the practice to prepare for Midland in two weeks."

I extended my hand. "In Texas, as you well know, a handshake is as good as your word." We shook hands, and I set out on my sixty-mile trek back to Brownwood, straight to the hospital to stay the night with my mother. I drove through a countryside permeated by the smell of longhorns, smiling over a trip gone well.

CHAPTER 8

Wednesday

After a restless night, I woke up in the hospital chair beside my mother's bed. I was stiff and a little slow to my feet. It was nearly six o'clock, and I had to get home to clean up, get ready for work, and get John's breakfast on the table. I kissed my mother, told her she had a great night, and reminded her that I'd be back around lunchtime.

A couple hours later, I was sitting in my office when I heard a knock on my open door.

I looked up to see my lifelong friend Alex Munroe dressed in a spiffy coat and tie, the first time in years I had seen him in something other than black slacks and a black-and-white-striped shirt.

"Seems to me this is highly unorthodox." I gestured for him to have a seat.

"So you know I'll be officiating your game Friday night," he said.

"I've heard. I haven't seen you since Daniel Baker College played at Howard Payne last season. How long has it been since you officiated a high school game?"

"I never have."

"This whole thing is new to me, but I can't say a ref visiting a coach must be common. What brings you here?"

"Look, Tylene, I've been put in an awkward position. The district asked me to handle this game because of my experience. They're worried it might get out of hand."

"Any game can get out of hand at any time. Be frank with me, Alex."

He hesitated.

"What is it?" I asked again.

"No high school refs would take on the game."

"Let me see here. The whole state of Texas, and they can't find a single crew to work our game? I didn't realize there were so many yellowbellies."

"It's not that, Tylene. It's just not a good career move, if you know what I mean."

"So what do you want from me?"

"I want to know one thing." He paused as if to gather his thoughts, to decide how to most diplomatically ask me his question. "Can you coach?"

Can I coach?

"I should be accustomed to this question, but you know what? I'm pretty tired and insulted by it. And I had expected more from you. You know me, Alex. You know my story."

"I don't mean to be disparaging. I just want to know how to prepare my crew. I have a responsibility to my men, too. And if your boys aren't well coached, there could be so many dang penalties, the game will last all night. I just need to know what to expect."

I stood up, signaling the end of the visit.

"Expect a high school football game," I said. I extended my hand. "Give my best to Judith," I added as Alex walked from my office. I had remained cordial, but I was seething and wanted nothing more than a little time to myself.

I closed my office door. Once I sat down, I leaned back in my chair, closed my eyes, and took a deep breath. In that moment, I was surprisingly relaxed, and I felt as if I could easily doze off, but I was startled when just minutes later, I heard a knock at my door. I was too relaxed to get up, so I shouted, "Come in!"

It was Mavis, and I hadn't seen her—not even walking the school's halls—since we were sitting awkwardly and silently side by side in church.

"I'm so sorry about Vern," Mavis said before she had crossed the door's threshold. "I specifically asked him not to bring it up, but he never listens to me."

"Mavis, I'm not worried about Vern."

"I hope you know I don't see things the way he does," Mavis said once she sat in the guest chair across from my desk.

"I just don't get it. After all you two have been through, he still sees it this way?" I asked.

"When we got that call—Vern's just never been the same,

Tylene. Nothing is ever good enough. Nothing is ever simply *right*."

For the first time in the nearly three years since Vern and Mavis lost their son during the attack on Pearl Harbor, I saw a depth of pain in Mavis's eyes I had not seen since the day she got the news. I could almost touch the hurt, as fresh as it was when the soldiers bearing the horrific news left Mavis and Vern's home. Emotions she had hidden so well were raw, and I wondered how she had managed to cope with a husband who had become an angry, isolated man.

"Tylene, I believe in what you're doing. A lot of women in town do, too, but we just can't say it publicly."

"I get it. I understand, Mavis."

Then I asked her if she'd like to watch football practice after school.

She hesitated.

"I can do that," she said. "Yes, I can do that. I think it's time. I know Jack would want me back. So, yes, Tylene. I'll be there."

THAT AFTERNOON, I was standing near midfield when the boys emerged from the field house and began to loosen up by jogging around the track. I watched them as they ran in a cluster, and as they rounded the home-side stands, I caught a glimpse of Mavis climbing the bleachers. When the boys rounded a second time and I had swiveled to keep an eye on them, I spotted Mavis sitting about six or seven rows up. I smiled, but I knew she was too far away to see it.

It was the first time I had seen Mavis sitting in the stands since Jack's last home game. I remember it vividly. Jack was smothering on defense that night against San Angelo. A middle linebacker, he must have accounted for upward of a dozen solo tackles and a dozen more assisted. He had San Angelo's running game so disrupted, the team started to pass in desperation. Problem was, the quarterback wasn't a passer, and Brownwood ended up with a lopsided victory. The final score escaped me.

Jack was the kind of player who couldn't catch up to anyone in the open field, but if he caught someone at or near the line of scrimmage—look out. He was small—maybe five feet, nine inches tall—but awfully strong. His senior season had been shaping up to be his best, but with three games to go, he separated his shoulder during a game at Post. Jack's injury did not require surgery, just a couple months' rest. The youngest of four children and the only boy, Jack never played football again. He graduated in 1941 and joined the navy not a week later.

"Speed it up, fellas!" I shouted to the team. The cluster began to move at a brisker pace, and the larger players dropped behind the pack. I was startled when I heard Mavis shout, "Move!" Her shout was in the direction of the linemen, lagging a good twenty yards behind. I figured Mavis had just been swept away with enthusiasm, but she kept shouting. Louder and louder.

"Don't get left behind!" she shouted. "Move it!"

At that point, I realized I had misinterpreted her enthusiasm. Mavis was angry and the anger intensified with each shout. I was confounded and uncertain how to respond, witnessing a side of Mavis I had never before seen. The boys appeared just as stunned. They had all stopped running. I could sense their eyes on me as I dashed up the stands to Mavis's side. I noticed she was sweating profusely, more than would even be expected under the humidity and direct sunlight of the ninety-degree central Texas afternoon. It was as if she hadn't seen me, even though I was at her side with my left hand resting on her right shoulder. She continued to look straight ahead.

"What are you stopping for?" she shouted to the boys. "Run!"

I put my arm around her shoulders, and she finally turned to me.

"I don't want to stop screaming," Mavis said to me between gritted teeth. "I don't want to be composed anymore. I'm sick of being composed. Ever since Jack died, Vern has shut me out. I've catered to all of his needs, but not once has he asked me about mine."

Tears began to stream down her face. Mavis pulled a handkerchief from her purse.

"I miss Jack," she whispered, her head down yet leaning toward my shoulder. I rubbed her back and said nothing. Together we walked down the stands and onto the track. Once we stopped, she dabbed her eyes and repeated, "I miss Jack. I miss Jack so much.

"I'm angry with Vern," she continued. "I'm angry that he's shut me out, and I'm angry that he's doing it to you and John now, too.

"Look at those boys," she said, pointing at the boys, who

had resumed running. "They're boys, for goodness' sake! It's not their time, and it seems like only you know that." Her voice again began to amplify. "What's wrong with these people, Tylene? How can they be so narrow-minded? It's not just football—it's life! My Jack is gone. I'll never get him back. But these boys, Tylene, it's just not their time."

"Mavis, not all these boys get it, either," I said. "I passed two of them—both seniors—in the hallway this afternoon, both former middle-school students of mine, only the three of us in sight, and they pretended not to know me."

Mavis put her arms around me. "You need to do this, Tylene," she whispered. Then she left.

Just minutes later, I was shouting at the cornerbacks.

"Stay low!"

"Your sets are too high!"

"Keep your body square!"

"Don't open your hips!"

"Keep your feet calm!"

"Be patient at the line of scrimmage! Don't give away any advantage we're trying to create! But get those hands ready to react quickly!"

My plan was to force Stephenville to throw as much as possible. We had to keep the ball out of the hands of their speedy running back, so our corners had to be ready.

I spent the next several minutes instructing the cornerbacks, having them take as many repetitions as time would allow.

"Once the ball is snapped, your hands come up," I said. "Using the proper hand, jam the receiver and disrupt his timing. You've got to make him run laterally. Align outside the shade of the receiver and funnel him inside."

I'm not sure if Mavis's behavior stunned the boys into focus or if they just had a shift in attitude with the game approaching. In any case, it was a spirited and productive practice.

Afterward, I stopped by the hospital only to discover that my mother had been discharged, so I headed for my folks' house.

"I see you were sprung early," I said to my mother, who was sitting on the living room sofa.

"I'm feeling so much better now, Tylene," she said. "I'm so tired of being in a bed, I just might stay out here on the sofa all night!"

She laughed. It was so good to hear her laugh. Dad was standing nearby, and I looked up at him. He smiled and nodded his head as if to tell me, *Yes, Mom's doing well.*

I then joined Bessie Lee in the kitchen to help her prepare supper.

"The doctor said she responded well to the treatments," Bessie Lee said. "At this point, it's just a matter of balance— rest, activity, rest. We'll just have to keep an eye on her."

"She seems remarkably pleasant for what she's just been through," I said.

"I thought so, too. And Dad's been Dad. Never a moment's rest."

We both agreed that that was a good sign. Soon after, I headed home to prepare supper for John and myself. I was exhausted. I had not slept well the night before, and the afternoon was especially hot. The sun's rays had beaten down on all of us like fire batons. Yawning as I peered into the oven, I was suddenly startled when the telephone rang.

"Miss Tylene?" the caller asked.

"Yes?"

"I'm calling from KDUX radio in Dallas, and I have a few questions for you. You weren't sitting down to supper, were you?"

"As a matter of fact, I was fixin' to. It's on the stove, so if I can be of help, I've got just a few minutes."

We talked briefly, but I cut the interview short, promising that if the reporter called me during my lunch break at school the next day, I'd give him more time. We hung up, and not a minute passed before the phone rang again. A reporter from San Antonio, requesting another brief interview.

"Maybe we ought to keep the phone off the hook for a spell," John said.

"I would if not for the boys. Never know when they might need me for something."

And yet again, the phone rang.

"Good grief," John said as I answered.

"Miss Tylene." It was Moose on the line. "They're serious this time."

"Stephenville?"

"No. I heard last Monday, shortly after you called your first practice, that the board had scheduled a secret meeting at the school tonight to officially cancel the season. I didn't say anything to you, because I was hoping they wouldn't go through with it. Got wind today that it's still on."

After we hung up, I sat down at the kitchen table with John and told him what I'd just heard.

"Moose said he had a plan, but he didn't fill me in about it," I told John. We then agreed on what we needed to do: attend the meeting. I turned off the stove, pulled off my apron, and grabbed my purse.

When we arrived at the school, we were surprised to see not only a packed parking lot, but Moose, standing among the sea of trucks and cars. Although he had said he preferred that I not attend, I knew he had been waiting for us to arrive. I could tell he had more to say.

"Let me have it," I said as John and I approached Moose.

"It's Jimmy," Moose said. "I'm not sure he's on board with you as coach. At least, I have reason to believe that he's not."

Taken aback, John asked, "What gives you that impression?"

"Yesterday morning I overheard a conversation between Jimmy and Bobby Ray. When Jimmy realized I'd heard him, he called me over, handed me a letter he'd gotten from Stanley. I still got it."

Moose pulled the letter from his pocket and handed it to me.

Hey kid,

They say I might make it home for a game or two, if you have a season, that is. I understand what you mean about a lady coach. I'd feel the same way if I was in your shoes. But I only got one shoe now.

When my leg got blowed off, I grew a brain. You want to play, you got someone who wants to coach you. What's the problem?

So she wears a dress. She knows the game, and she can kick ass. I'd give anything to be in your shoes. Both of them.

Take care of Ma.

Love ya, kid,
Stanley

"Sounded like Jimmy needed convincing, and I wasn't sure if it worked, so I dug a little deeper," Moose said.

I stared at the letter. It gave me a greater understanding of the depth of Jimmy's conflict. I didn't ask Moose what he meant by digging a little deeper. I just said, "Let's go inside."

Moose said he'd be in shortly. He was finishing a Lucky Strike and also wanted to visit the men's room.

John took my hand. As we began walking toward the auditorium, we saw a flash of light and heard the *poof* of a camera's bulb. We turned in the direction of the sound and were blinded by the flash of yet another photo being taken.

"This way, fellas!" someone shouted from among the cars in the parking lot. "It's the Tylene lady!"

Upon hearing this, I leaned into John. He put his arm around my shoulders, I tucked my head against his chest, and we increased the pace of our walk.

"Feels like an ambush," I said.

"Just keep walking," John said.

As we entered the auditorium, I was stunned by the size of the crowd. The auditorium was full—parents, grandparents, teachers, administrators, graduates, local supporters of the school and of the football team.

"How badly do they want me out?" I whispered to John. "All these people knew about the meeting, and word never made its way to me."

John and I slipped into seats in the back of the room. Mr. Redwine was sitting in the last row, about a dozen seats over from us. I wondered why he had distanced himself from the board. Making eye contact, Mr. Redwine nodded at me. I nodded back.

The room had a capacity of five hundred. The board was made up of twelve members—all men—who would later say they had anticipated a quiet vote. They sat at tables they had carried in from a small room adjacent to the auditorium. The meeting was called to order.

"We're here only to vote on the cancellation of the football season," said Buck Taylor, the school board president. "There will be no input from the crowd. Frankly, I'm not sure how the word got out or why y'all are here, but we're moving ahead. Voting only."

The crowd stood and cheered.

"We're here to support y'all," a man shouted.

"We ain't a girls' team!" shouted another man.

"Don't embarrass the boys!" yelled yet another man.

With every shout, the crowd—which I figured to be close to five hundred people, the vast majority men—cheered. Heads were nodding. People were whispering. Facial expressions revealed solidarity. *Certainly, I must have some allies in town,* I thought, but for some reason they seemed to have stayed home.

John looked at me. I had nothing to say. The entire display was disappointing but mostly hurtful. The town I'd grown up in, the team I loved, the boys I taught—all had turned their backs on me. Had they spit in my face, I would have felt no worse than I did as I listened to the shouts, the anger, and the vitriol.

"Let's get out of here," John said.

He grabbed my hand, and as we were about to stand and leave, a door in the far-right back of the room opened.

In walked the football team. Underclassmen dressed in street clothes and seniors wore their maroon-and-white game-day uniforms, BROWNWOOD splashed across their chests. Jimmy walked in first and shouted, "Hold the vote!"

Everyone turned. The whispers started: *What's going on? What's this about? What are they doing?*

As the underclassmen scattered among the crowd, the seniors walked to the front of the room, directly in front of the school board. All seven seniors faced the crowd. Jimmy, standing in the center of the seven boys, turned to face the school board.

"We know why you're here, and because you're here to cancel the season, there is something we want you to witness."

Jimmy then turned, and while standing among his fellow seniors, he faced the crowd.

"Most of us started playing football when we were in junior high," he said. "For years, we'd come to Lions games, dreaming of our turn, our senior year, wearing the school name across our chests for one last season. We have a coach, and if you hadn't noticed, she's sitting in the back of the room. Yes, *she*. But because that's not good enough for you, for the seven of us standing here, it's over. We are here to take off our Brownwood Lions football uniforms for the final time in our *lives,* and we want you to watch."

In unison, they took off their heavy leather helmets.

The crowd gasped.

They took off their jerseys.

The gasp got louder.

As they began to unlace their shoulder pads, someone shouted, "Stop!"

The seniors stopped and looked in the man's direction.

Then another man shouted, "Wait!"

Then the shouts started coming from everywhere.

"Hold the vote!"

"I can't watch it end! Not like this!"

Jimmy, Bobby Ray, Kevin, Charlie, Jake, and Willie appeared elated, when I noticed they all looked over at Roger Duenkler. Roger was the only senior who had taken his shoulder pads off.

Roger looked at the remaining six seniors and then at his dad, Moonshiner, who was gesturing with his head as if to say to Roger, *Let's get out of here.* The room went silent.

Moonshiner then stood up and shouted, "She's got y'all fooled! She forced Moose out, and I witnessed it. I caught her hiding out in the parking lot during football practices taking notes on everything she thought Moose was doing wrong. She hired him just to make it look good. She's been planning this all along."

Moose, standing in the back, shouted, "It's true!"

The crowd turned. I was shocked. I had never forced Moose out. I'd done everything I could do to make it work.

"You can't deny it, Tylene," Moonshiner said. "It's over."

With a cane in his right hand keeping him steady, Moose, who was known to use a cane only when extreme fatigue had set in, walked down to the front of the room and took the microphone.

"It's true, she was the coach all along. She was keeping her promise to me," Moose told the crowd. "I was in over my head, so she spent an hour and a half under the sweltering sun, keeping notes, so she could meet up after practice to help me. She mentored me. I was never the coach. It was always Miss Tylene, whether she knew it or not.

"And one other thing," Moose said. He paused and then walked toward the hallway door, the door the board had entered with their tables and chairs. Moose opened the door and the crowd gasped, and immediately I knew why I had been unable to reach Moose throughout the day. At the entrance sat Stanley in his wheelchair. His partially amputated leg heavily wrapped, Stanley slowly wheeled himself through the doorway. Moose stepped beside him and pushed him to the center of the room. Jimmy ran to his brother. They embraced, and both began to cry.

"Look at me," Moose said to the crowd. He then lifted his cane and hung it on his right wrist. "Look at Stanley."

Stanley was still in the embrace of his brother.

161

Pointing to the seniors with his left hand and holding the microphone in his right, Moose said, "We are their future." And then he paused.

Wiping away tears with the back of his left hand, Jimmy walked back and stood with his teammates.

"They are the present," Moose said. "Don't give them their future before they have finished with their present."

Despite Moose's plea, Roger walked up to his father, and together they approached me.

"My son will never play for a dame," Moonshiner said. He then turned to his son standing beside him.

Roger handed his equipment to me and then glanced back at his teammates, and I recognized conflict splashed across his face. I knew Roger tried to please his father, so I was disappointed but not surprised when Roger followed Moonshiner. Together they walked toward the exit.

"I'm with you, Moonshiner!" someone shouted. One by one, men sitting throughout the room began to stand and walk out.

"I'll have no part of this," one said to me as he headed for the exit.

"These boys would be better off hog-tied than playing for a woman!" shouted another. The discordant men gathered at the back exit. Moonshiner opened the door and they poured out, while inside we could hear in the distance the sound of a plane flying into our airfield. We knew another body was likely on board, this time carrying the remains of a soldier from a neighboring town.

At that point, with roughly two dozen men having left, the room fell silent. It was broken only when a handful of men who had just walked out opened the door and walked back in—the sound of the plane piercing their hearts, I figured.

Through it all, I hadn't noticed that Mr. Redwine had moved from his seat in the back and taken over the microphone. He called for attention.

"We just heard another plane flying overhead," Mr. Redwine said in a mellow and heartfelt tone. "Is there honestly any need for more discussion?"

Buck Taylor called for a vote. I could feel the tension in the room. The conflict. It cut through the remaining crowd like a knife into a melon. Torture.

The vote, which no longer focused on canceling the season but on proceeding with me as coach, passed—not unanimously—but once the final vote was counted, many in the crowd swarmed Stanley. I, too, got caught up in the throng of well-wishers, and for a moment, I forgot that I had just been officially named coach. A few minutes later, I was cajoled to speak, so I walked down to Buck, and he handed me the microphone.

I masked my emotion by remaining composed and kept my message brief. "Too many goodbyes," I said. "It's time we play some football. Thank you."

Just as I returned the microphone to Buck, I heard Jimmy shout out, "Lions!" The crowd joined in unison, and by the time Buck had gotten the room's attention, all he said was "Now let's get out there Friday night and support the team!"

Finally, once John and I had made our way out to the truck, and John got the motor running and the school was far behind us, I cried.

Thursday

I woke up early. I hadn't slept well, and when I arrived at school by seven o'clock, I was bristling and still frazzled by the events of the previous night. I parked and sat in my car for several minutes, gathering my emotional strength before walking down to the field to greet the nearly dozen men who had a week earlier committed to spending the morning preparing the field for the season opener.

I prayed for strength and exited the truck, and then I walked to the field. I thanked each volunteer individually, although I had trouble putting aside the picture in my mind's eye of so many of them excoriating me just the night before. Because I had administrative duties to tend to, I had asked Wendell and Moose to supervise the fieldwork, which included cutting grass, pulling weeds, and chalking lines. Before heading back to my office, I walked the field for a bit to survey its texture. At one point, I looked down and noticed my heels had sunk deep beneath the grass, and it triggered a thought.

I recalled that the rules of football allowed for a field's grass to be between one and three inches tall, and I figured the taller the grass, the slower the surface. Our boys had practiced only a handful of times, and they weren't quite up to speed. I pulled Moose aside.

"Have them mow down to three inches. Not a centimeter lower," I said.

Moose lifted one eyebrow, smiled, and nodded.

INSTEAD OF HEADING straight for my office, I stopped in on Mr. Redwine. I wanted to thank him for his support, something I knew was prompted only by our shared grief. But the moment I walked into his office, I knew something was wrong.

"It's Roger," he said. He slammed his fist on his desk.

"Please don't say," I said.

"Roger is a brave boy, but I'm certain his father had him by the collar."

"No, no, no, no, no!" I shouted. Through clenched teeth, I asked, "Why? Why did he do this?"

"One more year," Mr. Redwine said. "All Roger needed was one more year, but Gil has always had his own way of doing things."

"I am *so* angry," I said. "Why? Mr. Redwine, I just don't understand."

Mr. Redwine shook his head and handed me a tissue. I left his office in tears.

I WAS SO upset, I didn't get much accomplished for the next several hours.

By afternoon, I had pulled myself together. When practice was about to begin, I greeted the boys as they entered the field house and told them to put on the pads. I had to change my approach. Throughout the week, I had the boys work primarily on conditioning, technique, and skeleton drills, but with the game just a day away, the boys needed to practice in full pads. This was not ideal, twenty-four hours before kickoff, but I couldn't send them out there Friday night without any full-speed experience, no matter how brief.

Before we started, I gathered the boys at midfield and had them stand in a circle around me.

"Thank you," I said. I spoke slowly, pausing and swiveling to look into the eyes of each boy. "Last night, you reminded me—you showed the town—that we know something no one else seems to understand. We're a team. We *are* a team. But, as you saw last night, Roger left us. Boys, he also left town this morning. Mr. Redwine informed me that Roger took the early train to Dallas. His plan is to enlist. I wanted you to hear that from me."

I looked into the shocked faces of the boys. Jimmy removed his helmet and slammed it to the ground. I took a deep breath and let the thought rest. We remained silent, surrounded by the humming of the cotton plant. A few moments later, I broke the silence.

"Boys, we have a big game tomorrow. So let me tell you what I know about Stephenville. Their halfback, Red McNeil, can shuck the shoes right off a defender." I turned to our linebackers and defensive backs. *"Don't* be that defender. They also have a quarterback who can survey the entire field in a split second."

Just then, Bobby Ray's hand shot up. I gave him the floor.

"Mitch Mitchell ain't never played a down of A-squad football, Miss Tylene," he said. "Sat the bench all last year."

166

"That's right, Bobby Ray," I said.

"So how can you know he can see the field?" he asked.

"He plays piano."

The boys laughed.

"Anyone here play piano?" I asked. "Raise your hand."

No one did.

"Picture this, fellas. A young man sitting at the piano, his feet pumping the pedals, his right hand tapping out a tune, his left hand playing chords—neither hand going in the same direction or even doing the same things. And his eyes—where are they? They're locked on the sheet music. Now you tell me he doesn't have a finely tuned brain."

The circle stayed quiet.

"The boy can see the field, I can promise you that," I said.

I began to snap my fingers. "One." Snapping simultaneously on "one," I then said, "Two, three. One," snapping again on *one, two, three*. I looked at the boys and urged them to join in, which they all did. "One, two, three, one, two, three." As we tapped out the beat, I nodded my head to the beat of my snaps.

"See what I mean, fellas? He's got the beat. So how do we counter that? We go six to the bar."

"Six to the bar? What does that mean?" Bobby Ray asked.

"Technically," I said, "it's an irregular signature. It means unusual, odd, or complex. For us? It means unflappable. One step ahead. Try this." I counted faster, snapping my fingers on every odd number. "*One,* two, *three,* four, *five,* six. *One,* two, *three,* four, *five,* six. Come on, boys, *one,* two, *three,* four, *five,* six. See how much faster that feels?"

They didn't answer. They were too engrossed in the syncopation. I let them enjoy the beat, but reminded them that they were not only tapping out a sequence, they were tapping out our pace.

"Stay with that beat," I said. "*One,* two, *three,* four, *five,* six. Think fast. Move fast. Remain one step ahead. One beat faster. Remember, our style is similar to Stephenville's. But tomorrow night, we'll play *our* game. They'll play to *our* tune.

"For now, for practice purposes, we'll play a controlled scrimmage. We'll play as opponents, so don't be afraid to be aggressive. I'll let you know when it's okay to hit and when it's not, but if any one of you hits at any time I have called for a no-hit play, you'll be running the stands the rest of practice. Got that?"

"Yes, ma'am!" they shouted in unison.

I then huddled the offense. "H-crossbuck," I said. I stepped back a few yards and blew my whistle, and began to clap on every odd number. "*One,* two, *three,* four, *five,* six."

Charlie snapped the ball to Jimmy. Jimmy kept his feet moving like he was traversing hot coals. He turned to his left, faked a handoff to Kevin, then continued to swirl his body, checked off a receiver, and while parallel to the line, he handed off to Willie, who ran off tackle. Albert moved in and pounded Willie, knocking him to the grass just a split second after the handoff. I was astounded. It was the first time I had been so close to full-contact football, and I was overcome by the sound of bodies colliding at full speed.

From my seat in the bleachers, I had seen football as a beautifully choreographed game of chess, of wit. It was a thinking man's game, and the smarter man prevailed. But standing on the grass, choreographing the movements myself, I realized the true brutality of the game. Yes, chess, wit, smarts—but also strength, sweat, and pain.

With each snap, I could hear the crush—bone on bone, a chorus of elbows against jaws, knees against ribs. Leather-protected heads, but their noses and teeth and eyes were fully exposed. For the first time, I realized I both loved and hated the sounds.

To block out the noise, I focused on each play with the precision of a seamstress threading a needle. I didn't listen; I watched, playing Glenn Miller's "In the Mood" in my head to lessen the sound of the blows. After thirty minutes, I gathered the boys at midfield.

"No more contact. You have a taste of game speed, so now let's focus on assignments," I said.

I didn't want to wear the boys out a day too early, so with their pads still on, they spent the remainder of practice doing a walk-through. Once they were done, they assured me that their legs were fresh and that they were ready for Stephenville.

The boys, each down on one knee, circled me at the fifty-yard line.

"This is it, fellas," I said. "Look around. It's quiet. It'll look nothing like this tomorrow night. Now close your eyes. Think about what you see. Think about what you hear."

I gave them a moment and then I asked, "What does it look like? What does it sound like? Okay, boys, open your eyes."

I looked at them and shouted, "Are you ready?"

"Yes, ma'am!" they shouted.

"The place is going to be packed. There'll be newsmen, I hear from as far as Corpus Christi. We may not know entirely what to expect, but I can say with a fair amount of certainty that you *will* get heckled. Jimmy, what will you do?"

"Ignore them!" he said.

"What else?"

"Play football!"

"What kind of football?"

"Brownwood football!"

"Did you hear that, boys?" I asked. "Ignore the crowd. Play Brownwood football. And remember: Tomorrow night will be your night."

I reminded the boys of the pep rally and meeting schedule for the next day and told them to get plenty of sleep.

"You've been through a lot, boys, but here we are. We're still standing."

I walked outside of the huddle, then had the team lean in.

"One, two, three!" I shouted.

On that note, the boys yelled, "Lions rule!" They broke the huddle and ran to the field house. I walked to my truck, and just before I shut the door, I heard someone shout out my name. I recognized the voice.

CHAPTER 9

After a busy day in the office and a productive practice, I looked with great anticipation to a quiet evening at home with John. I had hightailed it to my truck and had just stepped in when I was called out by Moonshiner, who was hustling toward me. Once we made eye contact, he shouted, "This is on you, Tylene! This is on you!"

When he reached the truck, I asked, "What is?"

"My son is seventeen years old and headed halfway across the world to fight in a war because of you."

"Gil, I'm so sorry that Roger left. I've already been praying for him. But what are you talking about? I never wanted him to go. You know that."

"If you didn't want him to go, you wouldn't be coaching," he said. "You know I wouldn't let my son play for no lady.

Why didn't you just cancel the season? Why did you have to put yourself out there and embarrass us all? Embarrass the whole dang town?"

The thought of Roger going off to war sickened me. He was a boy. Maybe he was seventeen, but he looked not a day over fourteen. I wanted to cry for Roger, but in that moment, I was flabbergasted by Gil's accusations.

"You don't understand," I said softly. "I don't expect you to understand. But this one is on you, Gil. This one is on *you*."

I put the truck in reverse, backed out of my spot, and left.

Once home, I realized it had been at least a week since my last trip to the market. The refrigerator was bare but for a bit of leftover meatloaf. I warmed it up and whipped up some mashed potatoes.

John was unusually quiet during supper. I was clearly distracted myself.

"Moonshiner cornered me after practice. Said if I'd just minded my own business and stayed away from football, Roger wouldn't be heading off to war. Not now, anyway," I said.

"Blames you, huh? That SOB."

"John!"

"That just ticks me off, Tylene. That really chaps me."

I let a few minutes pass.

"What if he's right?" I calmly asked John. I pushed my plate, still nearly full, away from me and turned to John. "John, talk to me. What if he's right? I couldn't live with this."

John—now calm, too—took my right hand. "You had nothing to do with this. This was their decision. And without you, it may have been the decision of every other senior on the team."

I leaned my forehead into my left palm and closed my eyes.

"Are you okay?" John asked. "Is this starting to take its toll?"

"I'll be okay," I said.

I knew something was bothering John, too. I suspected business had been getting slower by the day, but I wanted him to tell me in his own time, so I didn't ask. We finished dinner in silence.

I began to pick up the dishes when John headed for the back door.

"I'll be in the garage," he said. The garage was his sanctuary.

After I cleaned up and washed the dishes, I grabbed my purse and headed to the garage, where I found John sitting at his workbench making fishing lures, a hobby he had long enjoyed. He said it relaxed him, helped him keep his mind off our troubles. I told John I was going to check on my mom and then stop by the football field once more to gather my thoughts.

After an hour-long visit with my parents and Bessie Lee, I pulled into the school parking lot. It was empty. I parked as close as I could to the football field, turned off the engine, and stared at the fifty-yard line. I allowed myself to reminisce about what led me to that moment, about what my father had taught me: *Every road in Texas leads to a football field. You pass by one, and you'd swear you can smell the leather of a well-worn helmet. You sit in the stands alone at dusk, stare at the field, and you can see the footprint of every football player who ever suited up, some so quick they left defenders in their stocking feet. Little kids grow up watching their favorite high school team and go to bed at night dreaming of their turn to play.*

I took a deep breath and hopped out of the truck, walked down to the field, and paced the sideline. I then stopped and stood at the bottom of the bleachers. As the sun began to set before me, I spotted the section my father and I had sat in when he had begun teaching me the nuances of the game: the upper corner, just right of the press box. I was certain the setting sun had cast a shadow that oddly appeared to resemble the two of us.

I climbed the bleachers, and as I got closer, I began to feel my father's presence and wished for a moment that he were there with me. I found our spot on the bleachers, sat down, and closed my eyes. In my mind, I could see the band standing at midfield, playing the school fight song. I spotted my childhood babysitter, Corine, playing the French horn. My favorite sounds began to fill my head as if I were hearing them for the first time.

Here come the Brownwood Lions!

I could see the boys running onto the field, hearing the cheers get louder as the team approached its sideline bench. I could see everyone standing: men in their ties, jackets, and fedoras; women in flower-print dresses, heels, and straw hats; children in play clothes and saddle shoes. I saw Shorty Wilkerson and considered gnawing on my nails.

Suddenly, I was startled by the sound of the field lights being turned on. I opened my eyes and saw the dim lights begin to warm up. I looked toward the field house and spotted a silhouette just outside the building's entrance.

"That you, Miss Tylene?"

"Yes, Wendell, it is."

I had not seen Wendell's face, but I had immediately recognized his voice. After all, Wendell was the town Yankee. He used words like *yous* instead of *y'all*. Or he added letters to words like *warshed* instead of *washed*. Sometimes he even changed a word altogether, like when he said ham and cheese was his favorite *sammich*.

"Didn't mean to startle you, ma'am!" he shouted.

"I'm fine. Just about to leave."

"Don't rush on my account."

A few minutes later, I walked down the bleachers and over to the field house.

"How does everything look?" I asked him. "Are we ready for the big game?"

"Yes, ma'am. I'm just doing a dry run. Don't want no surprises come game time."

I thanked him and turned away. Not two steps later, Wendell whispered, "Miss Tylene?"

I turned back.

"They're afraid of us, afraid of change," he said. He smiled. "Go get 'em."

I smiled back, nodded in solidarity, and headed toward my truck.

I DROVE HOME, eagerly anticipating my game-day visit with my father in the morning. But my enthusiasm was immediately squelched when I arrived at the house. I found John nervously pacing in the kitchen, arms crossed over his chest.

"What's wrong?" I asked as I placed my purse on the kitchen counter.

"Look at you, you're so composed, and I'm a nervous wreck," he said. "Damn Moonshiner."

"I shouldn't have told you."

"It's more than that, Tylene."

"Are you having second thoughts?" I asked.

"Yes, actually, I am. It's taking a toll on you, Tylene, whether you're willing to admit it or not. I can see the worry in your eyes. I can see that you don't sleep as well. You're not eating enough. You're often distracted. And I can't get last night out of my head. I didn't want to bring it up during supper, but we need to talk about this. If the game doesn't look good fast, they'll turn on you, Tylene. They'll turn on a dime. You might be strong enough for that, but I'm not so sure I am. Wednesday just confirmed it. I didn't see that coming."

"Now, John? You're going to do this now?"

"Tylene, I was down at the barbershop this afternoon. You're the talk of the town, and not so much in a good way."

"Certainly, that didn't surprise you. Not after all we've been through."

"No, it didn't. But the game is tomorrow night. Tomorrow night, Tylene. Our lives here are going to change tomorrow night, and I'm just not sure we're ready."

I sat down and folded my arms on the kitchen table.

"I'm not naive enough to think all eyes will be on the boys," I said.

"They're going to watch your every move, Tylene. They're going to look for reasons to mock you."

"Don't you think I know that?" I asked, snapping at John.

"I can't stand the thought of this town turning on you."

"So that's what you're expecting?"

"Look—the first three-and-out, and you'll lose the crowd. They wouldn't expect a perfect game from a man, but that's what they'll expect from you. Can you be perfect?"

"Stop it, John! Don't ask me a question like that!"

"I'm angry with myself for talking you into doing this."

"Don't be. If you hadn't, I might have just volunteered anyway. Look, John, we have to calm down. If we turn on each other the night before the game, then what?"

"I'm not turning on you, Tylene. I'm just so wound up. I had shaving cream all over my face, and the fellas were making jokes as if I weren't there. Made me wonder what they'd be saying if I *hadn't* been there."

I didn't respond. John sat down at the table beside me. Minutes passed, and neither of us spoke. He stared at me. He stared for so long, I had to break the silence.

"Please, John, not tonight. Please."

After a bit of silence, he stood up, and with that, the moment changed. He grabbed a bottle from the highest cupboard in the kitchen, just above the refrigerator.

"Is that what I think it is?" I asked.

"Walter gave it to me at the shop the night you left for Stephenville. Said we might need a swig or two later this week. Watch this. I'm about to break the seal."

I laughed.

John busted the seal, then reached for a pair of our delicate, hand-painted teacups, dangling on hooks just above their matching saucers.

"Not exactly what you'd expect for Irish whisky, but it'll do," he said.

"Oh, I don't know about this, John."

"A sip won't hurt."

He was right. It wasn't about the alcohol. I knew I'd only let the sauce dab my lips. It was about the mood. And it worked.

He poured a tiny amount into each of the two cups and handed one to me. He then lifted his up in the air and encouraged me to do the same.

"Here's to your first game."

We clinked our teacups and took our sips.

At that moment, we heard a knock at the door.

"It's about Stanley, Miss Tylene," Moose said.

CHAPTER 10

Friday: Game Day

Around three o'clock in the morning, I gave up trying to sleep and sat up. I didn't expect to wake up John with my slight movement, so I was surprised when I heard him say, "I think I'll get up, too."

"I might have dozed off for an hour or two, I hope," I said. "There's no way I'm going to get any more sleep tonight."

I started the coffee and we sat at the kitchen table, both of us still in our robes and slippers.

"I'm thinking I could make the pep rally this morning," John said.

"I'd like that."

"Nine o'clock, right?"

"Nine o'clock sharp."

The *Brownwood Bulletin* was still hours from delivery.

"You haven't shared the game plan with me," John said. "I know you have something up your sleeve."

I smiled.

"What is it, Tylene? The Statue of Liberty? A fumble-rooski?"

"No, no gimmicks. Just some solid football and a few decoy plays."

"Decoys? Nice."

I filled our cups.

"If the game is tight, I might go to Bobby Ray on a couple passes. I don't think Stephenville expects us to pass much, so I hope to catch them off guard. A deep pass or two."

"Deep?"

"I had them practice it a couple times. Jimmy's got the accuracy. It's just an idea."

John smiled.

"What do you think of a bootleg on fourth down beyond midfield?" I asked.

"If you think it'll work, my guess is it will," John said.

By the time the newspaper arrived, I was buried in my notes and mostly oblivious to anything else around me. Eventually, I noticed John open the paper and glance up at me. I could just imagine the headline, but I didn't want to know. John smiled, and I returned to my notes.

BY SIX THIRTY, I was heading to my parents' house. When I arrived, I was thrilled to find my mother sitting at the kitchen table. Bessie Lee was cooking bacon and eggs. As I had expected, my father was outside. The back porch faced east, and he seldom missed a sunrise. He swore it was the best part of every day. I grabbed a cup of coffee and walked out to join him. I found him visiting with Enrique Montano, not only his trusted ranch hand but his best friend.

Enrique was a rancher, born and raised in northern New Mexico in a small village called San Jose. He said he was related to nearly half the village residents and was hesitant to leave it twenty years earlier. But when Enrique's wife, Elena, passed away a year after the loss of their only child, he needed to get away. With limited English skills and few possessions, Enrique headed east on a two-horse buggy with no destination in mind. He didn't expect to venture halfway through Texas, but he said nothing "sang" to him until he hit Brownwood.

He met my father and began working for him, learning English and working alongside him nearly sixteen hours a day. Enrique insisted there was nothing else he'd rather do.

Upon seeing me, Enrique hugged me, wished me luck, and headed to the stalls.

"If I know my Petunia, you've been up the better part of the night," my father said as we hugged.

"I haven't slept much in days. I've also been doing a lot of thinking about us. Remember our first game together?"

"You thought I didn't know you were flipping that coin in your bedroom and running coast-to-coast with your doll," he said.

I paused. "I sat in the stands, Dad, last night at sundown. Thought you should have been there with me."

"Getting the lay of the land?"

"In a way. I really just wanted to remind myself of why

this means so much to me. You know, Dad, you changed my life with football. And it's not just the game I love—it's what it's meant to the two of us. It sticks in my craw when I hear men talk about football as a father-son experience."

"I guess the world ain't ready to talk about football as a father-daughter experience," he said. "But I wouldn't have it any other way."

"The world isn't ready for a lady coach experience, either, Dad."

"They don't know you like I do. But I also know why you're doing this, Tylene. The town may have forgotten, but we never will."

"Why is it that the pain never goes away, Dad, even after so many years?"

Just then, Bessie Lee peeked from behind the screen door and declared that breakfast was ready.

"I have to head to school. We just need another minute," I told her.

"Suit yourselves," she said. "Dad, you know you don't like your eggs cold."

"I'll be right there," he said.

"Any nerves?" he asked turning toward me.

"I think I've got them under control. Once we get that first game behind us, the scuttlebutt should subside, and we can finally sink our teeth into football."

"Tylene, I've been proud of you for many reasons. But this? This is different."

"Funny," I said. "Men do it every day. I guess I still don't get why the fuss."

I extended my hand to help him up. He got up slowly, as always, favoring his bad hip. He limped behind me, but insisted on holding the screen door while I entered the kitchen first. I had already eaten breakfast, so I left for school. I had a morning meeting scheduled with Jimmy at 7:15 A.M. and the team at 7:30.

WHEN I ARRIVED at the field house, I found Jimmy sitting at his locker, pumping air into footballs. I walked over and sat beside him. Each time Jimmy inflated a ball, he'd toss it into a basket placed a foot away. He had gotten through only two. He finished the third and handed it to me. Neither of us spoke as I looked down at the football I was gripping. Twice, I cupped it in both my hands, flipped it into the air a few inches high, and caught it. I was still holding on to it when Jimmy broke the silence.

"Excited?" he asked.

"I couldn't sleep."

"I've been here since six o'clock. You do know Wendell never locks the place up."

"Any second thoughts, Jimmy?"

"Not one."

"Is that what you plan to tell the boys this morning?"

"Yes, ma'am. I got my speech all written." He patted his back pocket to indicate where he had it stashed away. "I'm trying to memorize it, though. I think it'll be more powerful that way."

"You know, without you there'd be no game tonight."

"It really was Stanley, Miss Tylene. He knocked the sense

into me. Strange that it took a sailor with an amputated leg to remind us we were acting like fools."

"Did you know Brownwood canceled a football season once?"

"No, ma'am, I didn't know that."

"Nineteen eighteen. The boys should have been playing football instead of fighting a war. Like y'all, they were far too young. You have to do things when you have the chance, Jimmy, and not everyone gets a chance. When you do, you can't throw it away. You just can't." My voice tapered off into a whisper as if I were talking to myself. I tossed the football into the basket and stood up.

"What else needs to get done before the fellas bust through that door?" I asked.

"We're good. Nothing else, really," Jimmy said.

"I have to run to my office for a minute, but I'll be right back."

As I turned to walk out, I could hear Jimmy continuing to inflate footballs. I knew he had four more left.

FIFTEEN MINUTES LATER, I was back at the field house. Every member of the team had already arrived. Moose was sorting through the uniforms. Wendell was mopping the floor.

"Fellas, let's gather 'round," I said, using my right arm to indicate a circle I wanted formed around me. The locker room was small, so the boys clustered tightly, each down on one knee. I stood in the center.

"Finally, boys, the day is here. Excited?" I asked exuberantly, lifting my arms into the air, imitating the touchdown signal.

The boys started hollering.

"It's been a long journey to this day," I said. "Feels like a lifetime, not just a week. Tonight, we'll meet before the game and put the final touches on the plan. But now? We're going to get focused on what's in front of us. Come kickoff, we don't need any surprises. We can't pretend it'll be business as usual tonight. But we can put it on the back burner and focus on what we're here to do. We're here to play football. Now tell me, boys, what are we here to do?"

In unison, the boys shouted, "Play football!"

"And what does that mean to you?" I asked as I swiveled around and pointed at Bobby Ray.

"It means putting my best effort into every play, ma'am," Bobby Ray answered.

"What does it mean to you, Willie?"

"It means working as a team from start to finish, ma'am."

"And to you, Jimmy?"

Jimmy stood up to address the team. He began to reach into his back pocket, but he looked over at me and stopped.

"It means responsibility," he said. "And as captain, I have a greater responsibility to the team, to you, Miss Tylene, to Moose, and to our friends and family."

Jimmy cleared his throat, took a moment, and gathered his thoughts.

"I want us to begin our meeting with the Lord's Prayer," Jimmy said.

The boys bowed their heads, and as Jimmy said, "Our Father," the boys joined in.

"Amen," they said at the conclusion.

"Please, Lord, keep us—both teams—safe from injury, and may the best team win," Jimmy said. "I also want to tell y'all I've been thinking about something this week, about all the attention we're likely to get tonight because of Miss Tylene, and that attention is likely *not* going to be so good.

"I've heard the game atmosphere will be like a circus. Well, I ain't never been to no circus, but I've been to a rodeo. And I'm thinking the game atmosphere will be like a rodeo. We can expect lots of taunting, ridicule, and laughing. But like a rodeo, we can also expect awe—like when the cowboy stays on the bronc. In a way, we're like that cowboy. Tonight, we'll show Stephenville we can do more than just stay with them. We can beat them. I got a feeling we're going to surprise a lot of folks out there.

"So fellas, we can't let the attention get to us. We have to block it out tonight. We have to listen to Miss Tylene and to each other and to no one else. You got that? And if you do, shout with me: Lions rule!"

"Lions rule!" the boys shouted.

Jimmy looked at me. I knew he was expecting me to wrap up the meeting, so I thanked Jimmy and he sat down.

"We're ready. I know it. Go Brownwood!" I shouted.

The boys responded, "Go Brownwood!"

"Now, y'all have class in a few minutes, and then the pep rally at nine o'clock. Meet in the lobby outside the gym when class gets out so we can walk into the pep rally together." I then stepped out of the circle and told the boys to gather in closer.

"Lean in, fellas, and tell me who you are," I said.

The boys leaned in together and extended their right hands into the center, and as they lifted their arms in unison, they shouted, *"Brownwood Lions!"*

Shortly before nine o'clock, I was ready to lead the football team into the gym as the band wrapped up the final notes of the school fight song. From just outside the closed gym doors, I could hear Mr. Redwine begin his address to the student body.

"Good morning, Lions!" he said. The crowd cheered.

"Let's all get on our feet and welcome our football team and its coach, Miss Tylene," he said.

I heard the sound of movement on the wooden bleachers, so I imagined that everyone stood, and I could hear the cheers in unison.

Lions rule!

The doors opened. I walked in first, the seniors immediately behind me, with the rest of the team following behind them. Each boy was decked out in a pair of nice slacks, polished dress shoes, and his letter jacket.

The cheers continued.

The boys walked to their folding chairs neatly arranged on the gym floor, assembled directly behind the microphone stand where Mr. Redwine stood. Once everyone was seated, Mr. Redwine spoke.

"Let's please stand for invocation," he said, and the room went silent.

"Lord, we thank you for another school year. We accept the challenges you have placed before us as we prepare our boys for the unprecedented upcoming football season. We thank you for Miss Tylene stepping up to lead them. We pray, dear Lord, that our boys stay safe on the football field and that our entire school community stays in your graces. Dear Lord, we also ask that you keep our soldiers in your loving embrace and return them all home safely. Lord, in your name, we pray."

Once Mr. Redwine completed the invocation, the twelve-member cheer squad—six boys and six girls—began a rousing rendition of "Two Bits, Four Bits." Mr. Redwine stood at the microphone, waiting for the cheer to finish, and then once again asked for silence.

"It is with great pleasure," he said, "that I introduce to you our 1944 football squad. First, Captain Jimmy Palmer!"

Jimmy stood, and the crowd cheered. Mr. Redwine went on to introduce the boys individually, beginning with seniors and followed by juniors and sophomores. Each boy stood as his name was called. Once Mr. Redwine completed the roll, he turned and smiled at me.

"Last, but not least, I'd like to introduce someone we've all known for years as a teacher and as an administrator, who now has a new title: football coach. Please give a warm reception to the lady who will lead the Lions onto the football field tonight. Miss Tylene!"

The students applauded—if not warmly, then respectfully. As the applause slowed and the room became silent, a Winslow brother shouted from a corner seat.

"It's a bird. It's a plane. It's embarrassing!"

Immediately, a homeroom teacher approached the stands and signaled for the offending Winslow brother to come down from the bleachers. None would fess up to the outburst, so all three were removed from the gym.

Lula Ann, the student body president, then took the microphone to briefly address the crowd. She implored the students to conduct themselves with class and dignity throughout the game. She concluded by reminding the student body that Brownwood High School was known statewide for producing upstanding citizens, and she wanted the students to act accordingly while under the microscope of the Texas media. As Lula Ann spoke, I noticed the cheerleaders leaving the room, and I figured they were preparing for the pep-rally skit.

Following Lula Ann, Jimmy took the microphone.

"I really don't have much to say, except that we expect everyone to be at the game tonight," he said. "We've worked hard despite all the distractions, and I believe Stephenville will be caught on its heels. We can't do this without y'all, so please come out and support us. Lions rule!"

With that, Mr. Redwine informed the crowd that the cheerleader skit would follow. On cue, they emerged dressed as football players, save one who was dressed, I supposed, as me. The crowd filled the gym with laughter.

"Boys, boys, gather 'round," the female character said. She then pulled out an emery board and began to file her nails. "Let's play some football. Now, what is a football again?"

A cheerleader, dressed as Jimmy, said, "It's a ball, but it's not round like a basketball, and it has laces, but not like a shoe, and you catch it, but you don't wear a mitt like with baseball, and it can bounce, but you can't dribble it."

The female character laughed.

"Be serious," she said. "What does that have to do with feet?"

"Feet, as in football?" another cheerleader dressed as a football player said. "You can only kick a football on four plays: a kickoff, an extra point, a field goal, and a punt."

"Well, I'll be a monkey's uncle," my doppelgänger said.

"You mean a monkey's *aunt*?" asked another.

The crowd laughed so hard throughout the skit that I often had trouble hearing the lines. A part of me was embarrassed that my father was watching a skit designed to ridicule me, but at the same time, I enjoyed the entertainment, and I knew no one meant any harm. At the conclusion, Mr. Redwine asked me to speak to the crowd.

I approached the microphone, something I'd done many times throughout the years in my administrative role. But on that morning, and after that skit, I was nervous.

"Thank you," I began. I looked up at the bleachers packed with students—eager to hear what I had to say or eager for me to say it quickly. I turned to my right where John and my father were standing at the gym's entrance.

"I was five years old when my father took me to my first Brownwood High School football game," I said. I looked over at my father and signaled for him to come join me. In a suit and tie, carrying his fedora in his right hand, with the help of his cane in his left, he gingerly limped to my side. As he made his way to me, I was taken aback when the crowd began to clap. I smiled at the student body, and once my father was next to me, he, too, smiled and acknowledged the crowd. He hugged me, and we stood side by side.

"From the moment I saw the first coin flip, I've had Lions blood running through my veins. I was one of you long before there *was* one of you.

"I hope you know how much this school and this team mean to me. I want y'all to know I would not be in this position if I didn't believe I could get the most out of this team. In my short time with these boys, I've come to see that they can compete with the best the state has to offer. I'm fully convinced of that."

At that moment, I noticed a piece of paper circulating in the stands, and I sensed its distraction. Students chuckled as they glanced at the sheet and passed it on. I kept going.

"I want you all to remember the same thing I told the boys: A world away, there is a brutal war going on. Look at these seniors sitting here before you. They will be fighting in that war at this time next year—perhaps in the South Pacific, or even in Japan. They will be seeing things and doing things we cannot imagine. But their time has not yet come. They are here with us now. So please support them. We all hope for your support. We all need your support. Let's all come together tonight to cheer on your Lions. Now, let's get it done. Lions rule!"

The crowed followed up with the chant. My father and I parted, and I made my way back to my seat.

As the crowd cheered, Mr. Redwine marched up the stands and demanded to be handed the piece of paper. He returned to the microphone, dismissed the football team, and released the students to their classrooms. I stopped to hug my father and John, and then I headed for Mr. Redwine's office.

"I'd like to see the paper," I said. He handed it to me.

In my hand was a cartoon sketch of me hanging in effigy.

"Someone will be punished," he said.

I had seen the sheet circulate from left to right, and I knew who that someone would be: Mac Winslow. Shortly after I left Mr. Redwine's office, I ran into Mac between classes.

"Didn't have the courage to sign your artwork?" I asked him.

AT THE END of the school day, I was home for a couple hours before I had to be back at the field house. I wanted to freshen up and have supper. I didn't want to eat anything too heavy, so I cooked chicken soup with extra-large chunks of chicken and loads of carrots. Although it was soup, it had such a thick texture that it was nearly a casserole. John liked it that way. I liked it, too, but that afternoon, I didn't think I could handle much more than broth, so I set aside a small amount for myself before I thickened the rest for John. After supper, I cleaned up, washed the dishes, and jumped in the truck with John.

"I hear Dana Bible will be in the stands," he told me as we rounded a neighborhood corner.

"Oh, great. Not much more pressure," I said as I snapped on my mother-of-pearl earrings. "I've known about his interest in Jimmy. I guess I can't say I'm too surprised."

Just knowing the Longhorns' football coach would be in

attendance reminded me of the first time I'd met a UT football coach.

I was fourteen years old when one evening my parents and I stopped for dinner at the Underwood Café. Immediately, my father pointed out a stranger to me. The man was eating and writing something in a small notebook.

"Coaches the Longhorns," my father told me. "His name is Dave Allerdice, and he played football for Michigan not too long ago."

The Longhorns were coming off an 8-0 season, Allerdice's fourth in Austin. At twenty-eight, Allerdice was preparing to take the Longhorns into a newly created league—the Southwest Conference. The new conference was to be made up of Texas, Arkansas, Baylor, Oklahoma, Oklahoma A&M, Rice, Southwestern, and Texas A&M. Because of the proximity of the membership, recruiting had stepped up a notch, and we came to find out that Allerdice was in Brownwood to meet with the family of a local recruit.

Upon hearing of his status, I dashed to his table before my parents could stop me. I introduced myself and told him of my love for football. He then asked me if I rooted for the Longhorns. Too young to understand the value of diplomacy, I smiled and said no. I promptly told him my two favorite college football teams were those of Daniel Baker and Howard Payne Colleges. I asked him if he knew both schools were in Brownwood.

"I do," he said. "In fact, Daniel Baker will be coming to our place next season."

Next thing I knew, Coach Allerdice asked me a life-changing question.

"How can I turn you into a Longhorn fan, young lady?"

I just looked at him and smiled.

He said he'd leave tickets at the gate for my dad and me—in Austin, for the Texas game against Texas Christian. That fall, my father and I took the train to Austin and witnessed from midfield the Longhorns' 72–0 victory over the Horned Frogs. A week later, my father and I listened to the radio as Texas defeated visiting Daniel Baker 92–0. I remained a Daniel Baker fan, but the Longhorns were never too far behind.

Somehow, after having recollected so warmly that childhood moment, I let go of my anxiety over Coach Bible's attendance. By the time John and I arrived at the school, I was ready to get going. John walked me to the field house entrance, and he kissed me on the cheek.

"Goodbye, Stephenville," he said before he walked off.

Preparing to lead my own football team onto the field, I stood outside the boys' locker room, adjusting my dress, kicking dirt off my one-inch pumps, and looking at my watch. *It's fifteen minutes to kickoff,* I thought. *What's taking so long?*

Finally, Moose emerged from the locker room.

"They're ready for you," he said.

I stepped in. The boys were sitting beside their lockers, and I could feel tension as they sat quietly. They stared at me and then at each other.

Jimmy looked over at Willie, and in a voice loud enough for the entire room to hear, he broke the silence. "Hey, Willie, just ignore the dress. And the pumps. And the pearls."

Slowly the team went from suppressed laughter to full-blown hysteria. I knew they meant no disrespect. Although I had run each practice in similar attire, I was aware that the big stage would draw more attention to my look. And what a great way to break the tension!

I smiled and nodded, and considering we were amid an aroma of body sweat, dirty socks, and feet, I said, "And I'll ignore, shall we say, the fragrance."

Everyone laughed, even Wendell, who was placing footballs into a basket that was to remain on the sidelines throughout the game.

With the ice broken, I changed the tone. I gathered the boys around me, creating a tight-knit circle, and I began my pep talk.

"Young men, this is what we've worked for. I know this isn't the way you expected things to go, especially you seniors, but no matter what you might hear from the stands, I know you're ready. We can beat this team. We *are* going to beat this team! Now focus on your assignments. What are we here to do?"

"Play football!" the boys shouted.

"What kind of football?" I asked.

"Brownwood football!" they shouted.

I exited the circle. The boys moved in closer and more tightly and extended their right hands toward the middle of the circle. As they lifted their arms upward, in unison they shouted, "Go Lions!"

The boys broke the huddle and moved near the locker room exit. I stood out front. I shouted, "Let's go!"

The field house door flung open, and the team followed me, running out to the sounds of the band and fans screaming and cheering.

I had told the boys to prepare for a big crowd, but I had no idea I would see what was before us. Standing room only. Reporters packed the tiny press box, with the overflow shoulder-to-shoulder along the sidelines. As I walked, the boys ran past me, as I'd instructed them to do. I walked by reporters with name tags—reporters from Dallas, Houston, and as far away as El Paso—their pens and notepads at the ready. I overheard radio crews begin their descriptions as we streamed onto the field.

"Here she comes!" shouted Corby Rhyner, a radio announcer standing at the nearside end zone. "The Lions are taking the field alongside a lady coach. Miss Tylene, as they call her, is appropriately attired in a flower-print dress, heels, a string of pearls, and what look to be white clip-on earrings. I see no handbag, but it may be packed away on the sideline among the pigskins. We'll keep an eye out for it and will let you know!"

Knowing at any point my heels could get caught in the grass, I walked carefully, keeping an eye forward.

As captain, Jimmy began walking toward midfield for the coin toss, and because Moose had stopped by my house the night before to give me great news about Stanley, I waited for Jimmy's reaction with joyful anticipation. Jimmy walked faster and faster before breaking into an all-out sprint. He ran straight to Stanley, whom Moose was wheeling out to midfield. Stanley was in a Lions jersey—we had designated Stanley as the game's honorary captain—for the first time since he led his team to the state playoffs his senior season. He ran for 145 yards and three touchdowns in his final game.

When Jimmy caught up to them, Stanley looked up at his kid brother. I couldn't hear what they were saying, but by the look of things, Stanley had just told Jimmy that Moose had made it all possible. I saw Jimmy reach out to hug Moose before Moose began to walk toward our sideline.

Moose and I gave each other the thumbs-up.

Moose had driven up to the hospital to pick up Stanley for the Wednesday board meeting. But that was for just one night. What Jimmy had not been told was that Moose had made arrangements with Stanley's doctors to allow Stanley to return Friday night to attend the game. Moose picked up his former teammate earlier in the day. To see Stanley in a Lions jersey again was both glorious and heartbreaking.

I saw Jimmy hug Stanley and hold on to him for so long that Alex Munroe had to tap Jimmy on the shoulder. I knew Jimmy had to get focused, but I was thrilled that Moose had given Jimmy that moment.

I watched Alex prepare the boys for the toss, and my mind went back to the fall when Alex and I were Brownwood High seniors. It was 1918, the only year the Lions' season was canceled. Alex had been quarterback of the football team as a junior, but without a team his senior year, he became a volunteer for Daniel Baker College's football team. He did anything that was asked of him—running the clock, working the chains, keeping stats.

That season launched his officiating career. And because

I had no high school football team to cheer on that season, I also spent my Saturday afternoons rooting for Daniel Baker. I recalled it was the third game of the season when Alex needed someone to help with the chains for the second half of the Hillbillies' game against the Hardin-Simmons Cowboys. One of the chain-gang members had the flu, and by the second half, he could no longer stand up. Seeing what was happening, I jumped from my seat in the stands and offered to take the sick official's spot. I expected to encounter resistance. After all, working the chains is a vital role in working a football game. But Alex, who also was working the chains, vouched for me. Together we moved the sticks without incident. After the game, Alex thanked me for having done such a competent job. I said the same to Alex, choosing not to remind him that twice during the game, I had to correct his stick placement. Twice he had been confused on a third down.

Alex was about to toss the coin when I noticed the Stephenville quarterback and team captain Mitch Mitchell smile at Jimmy as if to mock him. As instructed, Jimmy kept his eyes focused on the toss, and, after winning it, he chose to take the ball. He then wheeled his brother to the sideline with the team, where Stanley remained throughout the game.

Next, I gathered the boys. I knew I would have to shout to be heard above the band, the cheers, and the Winslow brothers heckling from the front row of the Stephenville stands.

"Young men," I shouted. "We have to focus on what we're here to do. Don't let the hoopla get to you, or we'll be out of this before we get started. Remember, it's loud on the other sideline, too. But this is our field and our home. Don't look into the stands. Don't allow any distractions. We're ready to play, so remember your assignments. Talk to your teammates. Talk to me. Do what you're here to do. Now, let's play some football!"

Following the opening kickoff, the offense ran onto the field. As Jimmy huddled the boys, I could feel the energy.

The teams lined up. Immediately, the defense started to talk trash. I was close enough to hear it, but was praying the boys would ignore it. "Did your mama tie your shoes?" someone shouted from the defensive line. The ball was snapped and Jimmy was tackled for a loss. As the defenders got up from the pile, several laughed and taunted Jimmy. "Your mama needs to kiss your boo-boo!"

I was standing parallel to the huddle, and I signaled for the boys to run the same play. This time, among the taunts and laughter, the play worked. The Brownwood crowd went wild as Willie took the pitch around right end for a seventeen-yard gain and a first down. Unfortunately, Donald, the starting right tackle, turned his ankle on the play and hopped to the sideline. His replacement, Mickey, came in. I had told Mickey to tell the boys to run the same play.

Again, the play worked. Mickey had thrown a massive block on the Stephenville left tackle, allowing Willie to take the pitch twenty yards for another first down just across midfield. I treated myself to a tiny smile as I noticed the defenders had quieted.

But the next play had my blood boiling. Willie had scampered to the Stephenville five-yard line when I noticed a yellow flag lying on the ground near the line of scrimmage.

Alex had flagged Charlie for holding.

"Come on, Alex! That was a clean block!" I shouted. Alex then ran toward me and gave his version of what he saw.

"Ridiculous!" I told him. "Don't nickel-and-dime my boys!"

The half continued with both teams trading possessions with little success. The game remained scoreless as halftime approached, until finally we were threatening.

"Okay, fellas," I said, reminding the boys that on third down, they were just five yards from a touchdown. "We need to score. But let's run a decoy on third and score on fourth."

The boys looked at each other. It was as if I could read their minds. *What? Why would we waste a down when we're running out of time and we haven't scored all night?*

"Jimmy, fake a dive to Kevin, then pitch left to Willie. On fourth down, give the ball to Kevin. Snap on one, and just watch them wait on Willie. We'll be in the end zone before they realize what happened."

Just before the fourth-down snap, I saw Stephenville's noseguard shift about a foot to his left. Immediately, I knew Charlie had pulled off the four-pod, triple-quint option. I wanted to smile, but I waited to see if it worked.

It did. I glanced across the field and saw Coach Black slam his cowboy hat to the ground. With no time on the clock, we kicked the extra point and took a 7–0 lead. Then I smiled.

The boys cheered as they entered the locker room, but I quickly reminded them that as good as it felt to take the lead just before the half, the game was not over.

"Never cheer until a game is over," I said.

I had the boys clustered in the locker room and reinforced

the need to stay focused. "Again, assignments. Assignments. Assignments," I said. Then I turned to leave, telling the boys I'd be back in exactly twelve minutes, allowing them some time for privacy. I exited the field house and found myself nearly nose-to-nose with Mr. Redwine.

"Everything okay?" I asked, unable to suppress my surprise by his appearance at the field house.

"We all saw you shout at the ref on the holding call," he said.

"He was wrong. It was a bad call."

"And it was a bad move on your part, Tylene. You know I support you, but you can't be out there shouting at the ref in front of the whole town. You're the face of this team, and it's just not—"

"Not what?" I asked. I knew where he was going, but I wanted to hear it from him.

"Not ladylike," he said.

I laughed and shook my head.

"Well, thank you, Mr. Redwine, for not undermining my authority in front of the boys," I said sarcastically.

"Tylene," he said.

"Look, you can *scold* me all you want Monday, but right now, I've got a job to do." I turned away and began looking at my notes while I waited out the twelve minutes. I found myself calming my nerves by softly singing a few bars of an Ernest Tubb favorite, "Walking the Floor Over You," as I paced outside the entrance.

Shortly after, I entered the locker room to join the boys and lead them in our exit from the field house. As we approached our sideline, I noticed that the Winslow brothers had joined our fans on the Brownwood home stands. Moonshiner had shown up and was standing near the entrance. I also noticed that the standing-room-only crowd had grown exponentially. I figured people who had begun listening to the game on the radio had dashed to the field.

Maybe they couldn't believe what they were hearing, so they wanted to see it firsthand? I allowed myself a flash of satisfaction. I turned to my family and was stunned to see my mother hadn't left. She and I made eye contact, and she gave me a thumbs-up. John, my father, and Bessie Lee had equally encouraging expressions on their faces.

We began the second half on defense, clinging to our tenuous one-score lead. We exchanged a pair of three-and-out possessions, and I knew we needed to force a turnover if we were going to extend our lead or establish a hint of momentum. I paced the sideline, rubbing my forehead, thinking of my next move. I walked slowly at first, but as the game progressed I grew more intense. I hadn't realized how fast I had begun pacing until my right heel got caught in the grass. I jarred it free and then sent it airborne, nearly clipping a line judge upside the head. He turned to me but didn't say a word.

With one heel on and the other off, I limped toward the forty-yard line and retrieved my shoe. I pulled the other off my left foot. With my feet covered only in nylon stockings, I walked to the back of the sideline and tossed both heels into the basket of footballs where I'd also stashed my maroon-and-white handbag—one I had crocheted two weeks earlier in Brownwood school colors.

I stepped away from the basket and noticed the dirt track behind it. I bent down on one knee and started etching potential plays in the dirt. I had to think of something to generate an offense. The game was too close, and we weren't penetrating midfield.

A few minutes later and with less than four minutes to play, our noseguard Albert Brumfield tripped. He couldn't recover quickly enough, and Red McNeil dashed seventeen yards up the middle for a Stephenville touchdown. The extra point tied the game at 7–7.

"That's okay," I assured the boys. "It's tough to keep a team scoreless. We can get this back."

With possession and three minutes to go, I pointed to a play I had drawn in the dirt, turned to Jimmy, and said, "I know you can make this happen. I've seen you do this since seventh grade."

It was the Great Gatsby, a play so challenging it was rarely seen, especially by a triple-option offense. It was a go-to play, but it had to be run with perfection or it would fail. I knew it was one of Jimmy's favorite plays, and I had the boys run the play just once in practice, more for fun than anything else.

Bobby Ray had been blocking and running decoy routes throughout the game, and he appeared a bit winded. Now, he had to run his most important decoy route of the night and then follow it with what I had engineered to be the game-winning play. I knew he was up to the task; after all, he had been on the receiving end of four touchdown passes from Jimmy over the last three years. I'd seen each one of them.

Still without shoes, and with my glasses having slipped to

the tip of my nose, I stood parallel to the line of scrimmage, hands on my knees, eyes locked in on the play as the ball was snapped. My heart began beating faster, beads of sweat dripping from my forehead. The play unfolded just as I had hoped—Bobby Ray slowed to a stop on his out route, and the defensive back stopped as well. Bobby Ray was instructed to do the same thing on the next play, but after feigning a stop, he was to make a dash for the pass.

Preparing for the big moment, Jimmy huddled the boys together, then looked over his shoulder at me. He nodded so slightly only I could have noticed it. The boys broke the huddle and lined up.

"Hut!" Jimmy yelled. The ball was snapped, Jimmy faked to Bobby Ray, and the defensive back bit. The moment Jimmy pulled the ball back in, the defender slowed. Bobby Ray turned to his left, and with the unsuspecting defensive back thinking the play was not coming his way, Bobby Ray ran faster than a black-tailed jackrabbit. Jimmy heaved the ball downfield and hit Bobby Ray in stride. *Touchdown!*

I froze. *Did that just happen?* Although the crowd was rocking the stands, and the Lions sideline had erupted, I was so absorbed in the moment I couldn't hear a thing. Jimmy ran up to me, screaming, "It worked, Coach! It worked! Look at them!" He pointed to the Stephenville sideline. "They're in shock!" So was I. It was the first time a football player had called me "Coach." I was so overjoyed, I lost myself inwardly in the moment. But I had to regroup quickly, so I huddled the team seconds after Stephenville took possession and called its last time-out.

"We've done a heck of a job keeping their halfback in check, but he's their go-to guy, so we can't let up. Jake, be ready."

"I'm ready, Coach," Jake said. "I want him to come at me."

"Bobby Ray, you have much left in the tank? We still need you on defense."

"I'm good to go, Coach."

"We have to get off the ball quickly," I said. "I know you're getting tired, guys, but remember, no excuses. We have to force them into a second and long, third and long. If we do that, we might get a shot at taking the ball near midfield and running the clock out. You ready? Let's do this!"

I started pacing, now clutching a handkerchief I had grabbed from my handbag during the last time-out. First down. Stop. Second down. Stop. *Come on, fellas, third down. Let's get the final stop.* With my glasses blurred by sweat, and my soft curls drooped by the heat and humidity, I put my handkerchief to my forehead and began patting every bead of sweat, but for a few that had dropped from my chin.

"Let's go, men!" I yelled to the defense while clapping my hands.

"Yes!" I shouted as Kevin got off the ball quickly and was moving in on a sack. The closer he got, the faster I dashed along the sideline twisting and contorting my body, mimicking the play. Just as Kevin moved in on the sack, the quarterback threw the ball. Twenty-five yards downfield, Bobby Ray jumped in front of the receiver, high enough to tip the ball. As Bobby Ray fell on his head and back, the ball came straight down and landed on his chest, and he cradled it in his arms. Interception! We took possession at the Stephenville forty-five.

He wobbled to his feet, and I could tell he was hurt. I signaled to Moose, and we ran onto the field to help Bobby Ray off. I had instructed Jimmy to keep the boys focused on the sideline, but once I was back with the team, I called a time-out. It was our last time-out of the game. Stephenville had no time-outs remaining.

Bobby Ray went to the bench and sat down.

"Got the wind knocked out of me, Coach," he said. He claimed he was okay and was ready to return. I made him sit.

"Boys, we have to protect the ball," I said as we huddled. "We have the lead, we have possession, and we have time on our side. You know as well as I do that they'll try to jar the ball loose, so hang on tight. Don't let up."

"What about Bobby Ray?" Jimmy asked. "We need his blocking."

"He's done."

Bobby Ray heard me and jumped from the bench. "Done? Coach, I can go."

"Sit," I told him.

"Coach, we need him," Jimmy said. "He just got his bell rung. He can play."

"He's hurt," I said.

"No, he's not," Jimmy said. "He's just a little wobbly."

"Are you kidding me?" I said to Jimmy. "You think it's worth sacrificing an injured teammate for the sake of winning? Is that why we're here? To win at all costs?"

Jimmy just looked at me.

"I am not taking a chance." I turned to Kevin and shouted, "You're in!" As Kevin ran toward me, I told him his role was to run a solid route.

"Take the safety with you, away from the play," I said. He and Jimmy ran out and joined the huddle while Bobby Ray sulked on the sideline.

I was frantically shouting out formations with my arms flying side to side and up and down, indicating where the players needed to be. I pointed at Kevin, then signaled a slight shift to his right. He made the move.

On second down, Jimmy handed the ball off to Willie. Kevin began his route, but he was running too slowly and the safety wasn't fooled. The safety brushed Kevin aside and lunged toward Willie, knocking the ball loose and forcing a fumble recovered by Stephenville with one minute, two seconds to play. It was our first turnover, and it couldn't have come at a more inopportune time.

"It's not over. They've got a long way to go," I said. "We've held them to seven points all game, and we can hold them for the last sixty-two seconds. Stay confident, boys. All I ask is one thing, and it's the one thing I've always asked. What is that?"

"Assignments!" they shouted in unison.

Our defense took the field.

Stephenville began methodically moving the ball, chewing up the clock with long runs and a pair of ten-yard pass completions. With seven seconds to play, Stephenville had one more shot at the end zone from two yards out.

The crowd was so raucous, Stephenville appeared to have

trouble hearing its signals, because Mitchell began shouting out the plays louder and louder. Finally, on third-and-goal from the two-yard line, Mitchell took the snap, faked a hand-off, and ran into the end zone untouched. *Touchdown!*

As the clock hit zero, the Stephenville fans were cheering as enthusiastically as if they had just won a state champion-ship. But the Yellow Jackets still trailed by one. Just as I had expected, Coach Black sent the boys out for a two-point conversion try. I knew he wouldn't go for a tie with an extra-point kick. After all, a tie in Texas is no different from a loss.

I had already prepared the boys to defend the two-point try. They had run several mock attempts in practice, and I was certain the boys knew what to expect. Bobby Ray, who played a key defensive role in the practice drills, was begging to go out on defense, but I remained steadfast. Too risky. I went with Kevin instead. I watched Kevin line up and lock his eyes on Mitchell. Kevin then turned to me and briefly flexed his fingers as if playing out a tune on the piano. I knew it was his way of telling me, *I've got the quarterback.*

I held my breath as the ball was snapped. It seemed to happen so slowly, I felt I might pass out. I tried, but I couldn't exhale. I was too nervous to breathe. The defense had everyone covered, so Mitchell began to scramble. Kevin was moving in on a sack and appeared to have the quarter-back contained when the quarterback squirted through Kevin's grasp, ran to his right, and, as he fell, stretched the ball into the end zone just inches inside of the right pylon.

Game over. Stephenville 15, Brownwood 14.

Light-headed, I turned toward my family. I could see the crowd behind, standing motionless, shock splashed across nearly every face. Even the players looked frozen. My mind replayed John asking me: *Can you be perfect?* It was a paralyzing moment. And then the band began to play. The sound of the fight song filled the stadium. I'd never before heard the crowd sing the fight song after a loss. I stood at attention, just as all others on the Brownwood side had, and once the song ended, my father limped heartily to me. We hugged, and the crowd broke into cheers.

Lions rule!

The squad, about to begin the midfield congratulatory handshakes, joined in the chant, and I had to ask myself, *Do they finally understand why we had to play?*

Before I could acknowledge the crowd, I was swarmed by newsmen. I reached into the basket lying on the ground to fetch my belongings. Clutching my purse and heels, I attempted to break my way through the cluster. I begged reporters to give me a few minutes, but before I could escape the masses, I noticed the boys had already shaken hands with Stephenville and had begun making their way to the locker room. A few yards away I spotted Moonshiner. We made eye contact, but in an instant, he was lost among the throng. I knew Roger belonged with us, and I was heartbroken.

Eventually I made it to midfield where Coach Black awaited.

"You know I didn't cotton to playing against a lady, but I got to admit, you're a mighty fine coach," he said. "Can't say I seen this coming."

After the handshake, I headed for the field house. I was stopped a number of times by the newsmen, but I continued to ask each one if they would give me a few minutes to address my team. I promised them I'd answer every question once they were invited into the locker room.

About five minutes after the boys had entered the field house, I arrived. Moose was standing outside the door. As I approached, Moose cracked the door open, took a quick peek, then told me it was fine for me to enter. For the first time, I was outwardly nervous. I was trembling. *I let them down.*

I walked in to find the room eerily silent, and my stomach sank. But when I walked up to the boys, they stood and began to clap and shout in unison.

"Coach!"

"Whose coach?"

"Our coach!"

They repeated it three times.

Fighting tears, I turned to the boy standing closest to me and hugged him. It was Bobby Ray. And then Jimmy approached me.

"Coach," Jimmy said, "we nearly beat one of the best teams in the state of Texas because you know the game better than anyone in town. You persisted, and when you made Bobby Ray sit out the end of the game, it finally hit us. It never really was *just* about football, was it?"

My eyes welled with tears. I shook my head and whispered, "No." I couldn't bring myself to say anything more. Instead, I put my arms around each boy and hugged him as if he were my own son. Then I regained my composure and opened the locker room door. A trail of newsmen elbowed their way in—men with pens and paper, cameras and microphones.

"Miss Tylene, what was it like coaching your first football game?" a reporter shouted.

"How did the boys react to you after the game?" shouted another.

Before I could answer, I noticed over the shoulder of a reporter, off a slight distance, Alex was watching. I smiled and nodded my acknowledgment. He smiled, tipped his cap, turned and walked away.

"Do you plan on continuing?"

"What's it like to lose?"

I answered all and stayed until I was asked the final question by a reporter from Fort Worth.

"Miss Tylene, it couldn't have been easy. Why'd you do it?"

I gathered my thoughts for a moment and then replied. "No mother—no parent—should ever be left to wonder, *If only*. You see, *'If only'* is the cruelest of all declarations. If only I could have protected my son. If only I had my son for one more year or even for just three hours on a Friday night."

With that, I thanked the remaining reporters, and John and I made our way to our truck. My eyes were still seeing spots, and my ears were still hearing the *poof* of a camera's flashbulb. The parking lot was mostly empty but for Wendell's truck and the cars of a few lingering reporters.

John opened my door and kissed me on my cheek just before I got in. I was drained—physically, but mostly emotionally. Once in the truck, I sank into the comfort of our solitude.

As we entered our house, I walked to our bedroom. I sat alone at the foot of the bed, then reached down, opened the left bottom dresser drawer, and pulled out a small hand-carved wooden box, a box I had not opened since I had neatly tucked it away the summer of 1927—seventeen years ago. With the unopened box resting on my lap, I looked up and saw John standing within the frame of our bedroom door. He walked in and sat beside me.

I opened the box and took out the only pair of white infant booties I had ever crocheted. They had never been worn. I clutched them to my chest and closed my eyes. John wrapped his left arm around my shoulders and asked, "What position do you think Billy would have played?"

ACKNOWLEDGMENTS

It is with immense gratitude that I thank and acknowledge the following for helping me pull this novel together: Jean Van Waters, Diane Les Becquets, Ben Nugent, Jean Telarik Yodice, Dallas Huston, Mitch Moore, Mike Redwine, the librarians at Brownwood High School, Howard Payne University, the Brownwood Public Library History and Genealogy Research Branch, Davis-Morris Funeral Home, the Reverend Richard Hetzel, Andrea Somberg, Lucia Macro, Shane Bevel, and everyone associated with the Mountainview MFA program.

I'd like to thank my sister, Angela Butkus, for listening to my stories for all these years and my parents, William and Corine Herrera, for their love, support, and encouragement. I'd also like to thank my siblings Judy Baird, Monica Lazzara, and Bill Herrera.

And for putting up with me every day, I'd like to thank my husband, Chuck Lewis, and my daughters, Monica (and son-in-law Jake) Kirkendoll and Katharine Lewis. What made this journey extra special is that you were with me along the way. I love you all.

About the author

About the book

Insights,
Interviews
& More . . .

Meet
Marjorie Herrera Lewis

Shane Bevel

MARJORIE HERRERA LEWIS knew early on that she wanted to be a sportswriter. After several years at small newspapers, at age twenty-seven, Marjorie began working at the Fort Worth *Star-Telegram*. Two years later, she was a beat writer—working with veteran beat reporter David Moore—for the Dallas Cowboys. Marjorie later joined the *Dallas Morning News* sportswriting staff. Throughout her career, Marjorie covered college and professional sports, including the Texas Rangers and Dallas Mavericks, as well as tennis and golf. She also covered the Super Bowl, Wimbledon, the NCAA men's basketball tournament, and several college bowl games.

After researching and writing her debut novel, *When the Men Were Gone,* Marjorie became inspired by her heroine Tylene's journey, and she developed a burning desire to coach football herself. She was added to the Texas Wesleyan University football coaching staff on December 7, 2016. Marjorie worked with defensive backs on the field and with the entire team as an academic adviser.

Marjorie holds BS, MA, and MFA degrees. She says that Arizona State University prepared her to be a sportswriter, the University of Texas at Arlington prepared her to be a university professor, and Southern New Hampshire University prepared her to be a novelist. Marjorie is married, and she and her husband, Chuck, have two grown daughters and one son-in-law. ↝

Why I Wrote About Tylene

I've often been asked how I came across the story of Tylene Wilson, a woman who coached football in Brownwood, Texas, during World War II. My answer is simple: serendipity.

After decades of cajoling by my allergy doctor, I finally relented and scheduled myself for allergy-shot testing. My nurse, Jean Van Waters, commented on the T-shirt I was wearing, which declared me a Tulsa Golden Hurricane football fan. "I'm a football fan, too," Jean said. "The women in my family all love football. Probably because my great-aunt was a football coach during World War II." I just about fainted. Harkening back to my days as a sportswriter, I began a stream of questions.

By the time my head had stopped spinning and my adrenaline had stabilized, I stopped asking questions and just let Jean talk. The more she told me about her great-aunt, the more the story resonated with me. I began to believe I was the only one who could tell Tylene's story with any level of authenticity. In a way, I had lived a similar story, only forty years later and not as a coach but as a sportswriter. Tylene and I had both walked into life experiences we had not sought out, and in many ways we had not been welcome.

I was a sportswriter for the *Fort Worth Star-Telegram* when in 1986 I was asked to temporarily cover the Dallas Cowboys beat during the off-season. My job was to monitor the beat—handle any press announcements, stop by the training facility to see if anything interesting was going on, and check up on any contract talks or free-agent signings. But I loved the thrill of competition, so I set out to develop sources and break stories. I broke a few that caught the attention of my sports editor, Bruce Raben. Bruce liked my tenacity, so he handed the full-time beat to me. What he did not know at the time was that I didn't want the beat. And the first person to find out was Cowboys general manager Tex Schramm.

I was in the Cowboys public relations office of Greg Aiello when Tex stopped by. He said he'd heard I'd been given the beat. Always the proud Cowboys executive, Tex asked me how it felt to be a beat writer for the best team playing the best sport in the world. My honest reply was not well received. "I prefer college football," I told him. "I didn't ask for this assignment, and I'd rather not have it." His face became fireball red, and I realized that perhaps honesty wasn't valued as highly as I'd expected. He went on to tell me I was a fool. When he finished scolding me, I asked him why he cared so much. "Does the idea of a twenty-nine-year-old woman, five feet, two inches, give you comfort? Because if my appearance leads you to believe I'm a pushover, you do know you'd be wrong."

From then on, Tex, Coach Tom Landry, and all the other coaches and staff members treated me respectfully and professionally. One football player, however, had a different point of view, ▶

Why I Wrote About Tylene (*continued*)

and he was eager to share it. I was covering my first training camp at California Lutheran College in Thousand Oaks, California, when I walked from the field at the end of practice alongside a free-agent linebacker who turned to me and said, "You don't belong here." I looked at him and said, "I've seen you practice, and I'll be here a lot longer than you will." He was cut the next day, and I never saw him again. Despite his point of view, at least that football player was honest, and frankly, I appreciated it.

Like Tylene, I had grown up a football fan and had learned the game from my father, William Herrera. Like Tylene, I did not seek my job. And like Tylene, I endured ridicule, even from someone I had thought of as a friend. Tylene's story resonated with me because we were both unwitting trailblazers. And like Tylene, I had a backstory.

As we see in the book, Tylene wanted the boys to play football—not because she wanted to coach them, but because she didn't want them to lose their youth prematurely, as her son had. Her son, Billy, died only minutes after his birth. He would have been a senior in high school during the season that Tylene became coach. As Tylene's grandniece Jean told me, Tylene and John desperately wanted to have children.

I, too, endured a private personal struggle—one my colleagues did not know about—while covering the Cowboys. I, too, wanted to become a mom. I had a miscarriage early on, and while I was a Cowboys beat writer, I had undergone surgery that left my husband, Chuck, and me with no more answers than before it. I was also hospitalized on three occasions—the last time, I awoke to find my husband at the foot of my bed telling me he could no longer stand to see me suffering. He said it was time that we forget about becoming parents. It was a chilling moment.

Although we eventually had two daughters, I understand Tylene in many ways. I believe Tylene's life must be memorialized. Tylene was a woman whose life transcended football, who discovered what she was capable of even when she didn't seek it, and who brought joy to a grieving town during a time of war, even if only for three hours on a Friday night.

This is why I am telling her story. ∾

Why I Became a Football Coach

I became a football coach for one reason: Tylene inspired me.

Like Tylene, I never expected to be a football coach, nor did I grow up with the desire to become one. But as I researched and wrote Tylene's story, I realized that she and I possessed many similar traits, and I thought, *Wow, I'd like to do this, too.* Like Tylene, I love teaching and contributing to the growth and development of our next generation. And like Tylene, I love football. So in December 2016, I reached out to Texas Wesleyan University, a small school that was resurrecting its football program.

Texas Wesleyan had last played football in 1941. Shortly after the attack on Pearl Harbor, many of the team members opted to enlist in the U.S. Armed Forces, leaving college and football life behind. As a result, the program disbanded.

Under the bold leadership of university president Fred Slabach, Wesleyan revived its football program in the fall of 2016, beginning with its initial red-shirt class—a group of committed young men who would lay the foundation for the school's 2017 football season debut.

When I learned that Texas Wesleyan University was looking to add to its coaching staff, I contacted the head coach. I made it clear that because I respect the journey he and his coaches had taken to develop their careers, I would volunteer for a season and earn my way after that.

I was appointed to the coaching staff—one of seven volunteers—on

December 7, 2016, the date that also changed the trajectory of Tylene's life, and I had the honor of taking the field with the team when they played their first home game before roughly five thousand fans, seventy-six years after they had played their last game.

A reporter told me his research confirmed that I was the only woman in the country coaching at any level of college football that season. I was taken aback. And then I thought of Tylene. I wondered what she would think of my experience, many decades after she so bravely took on a task far beyond the gender expectations for a woman in the 1940s. She would discover that much had changed . . . and much had not.

Like we see in Tylene's story, she had the support of her husband, John. I, too, was enthusiastically supported by my husband, Chuck. Tylene loved Brownwood High School and had the support of its principal. I love Texas Wesleyan University, and I had the support of Fred Slabach as well as Steve Trachier, the school's athletic director. The football players came to respect Tylene. I, too, felt the respect of the young men on our team, young men who responded to me without qualm regarding my gender and my role in their instruction. Because of what I saw in these young men, I truly believe that women in football—and not just in football—will be more warmly welcomed in male-dominated fields.

But I would be remiss if I did not tell my whole story, and this is where ▶

9

Why I Became a Football Coach *(continued)*

Tylene's experience and mine converge on the negative side. As her story shows, Tylene was criticized and dismissed by some who did not appreciate her involvement in football. I, too, had that experience.

First, however, I must say that I worked directly with the defensive backs coach, Quincy Butler, a man of honor, knowledge, and passion for football and for his players. I learned so much by working with Quincy—not only about how to coach defensive backs, but also how to relate to young football players. Quincy, a former NFL defensive back and an All-Conference cornerback while at TCU, was a players' coach, someone whom young men could look up to. Football needs—and the football world should demand—there always be a place for the Quincy Butlers among us.

Unfortunately, I sensed that, unlike Quincy, the head coach and the defensive coordinator did not know how to best utilize my skills, and despite my many suggestions, they did not appear interested in figuring it out.

Still, their dismissiveness did nothing to diminish my love for Texas Wesleyan University, a gem in the heart of Fort Worth. I will be forever grateful for having had the opportunity to be a part of such a historical season, and I look forward to more women following in Tylene's footsteps. ᗧᘎ

Author Q&A

Q: Marjorie, some of our readers might be surprised to discover that Tylene Wilson is not an invention of your imagination! What brought you to tell her story?

A: Telling Tylene's story, for me, was a result of my own life experiences. I don't think I could have told her story had I not known what it was like covering college and professional football during a time that a woman in a sports department was extremely rare. So when I discovered Tylene's story from her own grandniece, I instantly fell in love with it.

Although by the time I discovered what Tylene had done during World War II, she had already passed on—a result of Parkinson's disease, in 1992 at the age of eighty-eight. John had spent many years caring for her throughout her illness, but he predeceased her. I wish every day that I'd had the chance to meet her, but I loved this journey of discovering her life story. She was an incredible woman.

Q: How did you draw on your imagination to tell Tylene's story? Do you feel you struck the right balance between what was true and what your imagination created?

A: I created the novel based on many core truths. Tylene and John did know each other for eleven years before they married, and they waited because she wanted to further her education first. She also did ▶

Author Q&A *(continued)*

work in a small office up a winding staircase above John's auto shop, and she did keep the shop's books.

   Among other core truths: Tylene was a teacher and administrator. Tylene was taught football by her father when she was a young girl. Her father was injured in the 1909 Zephyr tornado, and years later, he died as a result of the injuries he had sustained. Tylene's mother was ill in 1944 and died a year later. Tylene drove a truck, loved pecan pie, loved football and baseball, and grew up on a ranch. Her college minor was voice. John's hobby was making fishing lures. She and John wanted dearly to be parents. John also loved football, and together, after the invention of television, they would watch football broadcasts with the sound off. When their grandniece Jean once asked them why they turned down the sound, John's reply was: "We don't need someone telling us what we already know."

   I framed the story based on these core truths. I did so because after having completed my research, I realized there were too many dead ends. The story had been lost to time. I could have let it go, or I could novelize her life. I felt it was a story that needed to be told, so I fictionalized the accounts based on so many core truths.

Q: *How do you think Tylene's story would be different if she were living today?*

A: She was far ahead of her time. John was also ahead of his time in his support for her—not only her desire to postpone marriage to pursue higher education but her willingness to coach football in the 1940s. What strength that took from both of them!

What I think would be different today is the household gender expectations. As we see in the story, John was supportive, but it would not have occurred to him to do the dishes when Tylene was in a hurry. Instead, he'd offer to drive her through back roads he was familiar with. We never see John cook dinner. It wasn't something a man would do in the 1940s. We would see that today.

What I do think would be different today in regard to her coaching football is that Tylene would find this generation of young men more open to women in football than they were seventy years ago. My experience has told me that because Tylene knew her stuff, the young men would be eager to learn from her and play for her.

I truly believe that with women coming up the ranks in football, we will see a shift in their role—not only on the field but in the media as well.

Q: *Tylene seems like a very unique woman to her time—do you think this is the case, or do you think circumstances made her so?*

A: Tylene was such a unique woman in her time that had she not been, she could not have been prepared to deal with the circumstances she faced. She had spent her life preparing for that moment—she just didn't know it.

She also married a man who knew she was different—pursuing a master's ▶

Author Q&A *(continued)*

degree at night and during the summers, all the while staying devoted to her students. And what an arm! She could throw a football—and a baseball!—with the best of them.

Q: *John seems very supportive of Tylene and her choices—in what ways does their marriage resemble a marriage of today? In what ways is it different?*

A: Their marriage reminds me a lot of mine. What's different is that my husband helps out with the household chores. Full disclosure: He handles most of them. John did not. But that wasn't on men's radar in the 1940s.

John never went to college. He worked on cars. It's hard to imagine that he'd come home and fix dinner while his wife was off coaching a football team. It just wouldn't have happened then.

But he was so supportive that he was willing to risk his own livelihood just to support her journey. He dearly loved Tylene.

Q: *You were a football coach yourself, which is groundbreaking in its own way. What was your journey like?*

A: Like Tylene's experience, I, too, had ups and downs. But the ups far outweighed the downs, so much so that when the alarm would go off at 4:30 A.M., I'd jump out of bed with a spring in my step. And I'm a night owl! I remember telling one coach that with practices at 6:00 A.M., I was more likely to arrive having not yet gone to bed. I did that, too, a few times.

I loved working with the young men. It was a tough season—we were winless, although we received a forfeit after the completion of the season, so we finished 1-10. We never experienced the joy of victory, and that was disappointing, given all the work put into the season. But the young men never gave up. Working with them was pure joy.

Q: Football is such a Texas sport! What do you think creates the connection between Texas and football?

A: I didn't grow up in Texas. I was born and raised in Santa Fe, New Mexico, but my family spent vacation time in Dallas when I was twelve years old. I decided then that, when I grew up, I would make Texas my home. I fell in love with the people. I thought they were kind and friendly. Everywhere we went in Dallas, I felt a sense of community. It seemed no one was a stranger.

And that's what I think makes football in Texas special. It's about community. There are so many small towns in such a huge state that football fields have historically been the largest gathering spot in any locale. Link the toughness of the sport and the desire for hometown pride, and the combination makes for a perfect storm.

Author Q&A *(continued)*

Q: Have you been to Brownwood? How is its team doing today?

A: When I first heard that Tylene had coached football in Texas, I was thrilled. When I heard it was in Brownwood, I was ecstatic. You can't help but think of Brownwood when you think of football in Texas. Brownwood is one of the state's most iconic football towns, thanks largely to Brownwood High School's Hall of Fame coach Gordon Wood, who led the Lions to seven state championships from 1960 to 1981. The Lions finished the 2017 regular season with a record of 6-5.

Although I've never attended a Lions football game, I have been to Brownwood, and not just to research Tylene's story. I covered a football game for the *Dallas Morning News* in the 1990s at Howard Payne University, Tylene's alma mater. I remember the press box lost power to its phone hookups, and I had to go to the local hospital to transmit my story. They were great in allowing me to use a telephone! Afterward, my husband, daughters, and I made a beeline for barbecue at Underwood's Café. I have nothing but fond memories of my time spent in Brownwood. ∾

Discover great authors, exclusive offers, and more at hc.com.